Table of C

Hawthorne

Secrets Unveiled

Zayn Jamshaid

Published by Zayn, 2024.

HAWTHORNE

First edition. April 9, 2024.

Copyright © 2024 Zayn Jamshaid.

ISBN: 979-8224117505

Written by Zayn Jamshaid.

Thank you, Baba.

1 - A Guy Named Alex

My name is Alex, Alex Hawthorne, and let's just say I've had my fair share of moments where I didn't quite have all the smarts. Everhaven City—that's where I hung my hat. Used to be a real gem, you know? Everywhere you looked, there was a glimmer of hope, a touch of magic. I loved that place.

I worked as a journalist for the 'Everhaven Chronicles.' Not to toot my own horn, but I was pretty decent at my job. Uncovered some pretty gritty stuff, but I also made sure to shine a light on all the good in the city. It was a peaceful time, you know? Felt like we were really making a difference.

Then things took a dark turn. Mayor Carter Fairweather, bless his soul, passed away during the election. It was like a punch to the gut, the whole city reeling from the shock.

The people of the city started getting scared, scared of getting robbed, scared of being of a certain faith. So, they turned to hate.

Suddenly, that peace we'd fought so hard for felt like it was slipping through our fingers. And then, out of the turmoil, came Richard Caidwall, one of the guys vying for Mayor. He painted this picture of Everhaven reclaiming its glory days under his watch, a lot of people fell for it and he became mayor.

but you know how it is when you've got that gut feeling? Mine was telling me we were in for a rough ride, despite all the fancy promises.

I was sitting in my office, just thinking about the state of the city that I once cherished. My boss, Ronnie Coleman entered, "Hawthorne, what's wrong?" He asked, "Nothing much, Caidwall's doing a speech today in Haven Square. Are we heading over?" I asked, my voice tinged with exhaustion. Ronnie let out a sigh. "Yeah, Caidwall's dishing out promises left and right." I glanced over at Ronnie. "Then we report on it, like we always do," I said, pushing myself up from my seat.

An hour later we arrived at Haven Square. Haven Square was the heart of our city; parades, music, and peace. This is also where Fairweather was elected as Mayor.

"As Mayor, I will make sure Everhaven will have its peace again!" Caidwall yelled into the microphone, the crowd cheered. "As Mayor, I will make sure that criminals won't run our streets anymore!" The crowd cheered again, "As Mayor, I will make sure that the peace that Mayor Fairweather fought valiantly for, won't be in vain!" The crowd roared.

As Caidwall lowered the microphone and made his way down the stairs, the press erupted with clamor, waving hands and shouting for attention. "Alright, alright, I'll do my best to answer everyone," he reassured them with a smile. His gaze landed on a reporter from the Everhaven Times. "Hey there, what's your name, sweetheart?" he asked, pointing to the young woman amidst the crowd.

"Hello, sir. Evelyn Stoneheart here, reporting for the Everhaven Times. During your speech, you mentioned initiatives to reduce gas emissions prices and alleviate the overall cost of living. Could you elaborate on your plans to achieve these goals?" She said with a thick British accent as she began to hold her notebook. Caldwell for some reason hesitated but began speaking.

"Hello, Ms. Stoneheart. Thank you for your question, and let me just say, it's great to see such active engagement from our local press. Now, let's dive into it. Our strategy centers on ushering in a new era of sustainability and efficiency. We're talking about bringing in cleaner, greener energy sources and revamping our transportation infrastructure to cut down on emissions and make commuting a breeze. But we're not stopping there. We're also looking into initiatives like affordable housing and job creation to tackle the broader issues affecting our residents' cost of living. It's all part of a comprehensive approach aimed at enhancing the well-being of the entire Everhaven community." Caidwall proudly says. As the press clamored for his attention once more, he singled out a male reporter amidst the crowd. "Hey there, I'm Jake Reacher from Haven Forever," the reporter announced. "Can you share with us your plans for getting more involved in the Everhaven community?"

"Hello, Mr Reacher. Thank you for your question. Community involvement is one of the forefronts of my agenda. We're looking at a range of initiatives aimed at fostering stronger connections within Everhaven. From neighborhood clean-up projects to town hall meetings, we're committed to engaging with residents on a personal level. Additionally, we're exploring partnerships with local organizations and businesses to create opportunities for collaboration and mutual support.

Our goal is to build a community where every voice is heard and every individual feels empowered to make a difference."

The press erupted into a frenzy once more, and I saw my chance, raising my hand amid the chaos. Caidwall's gaze found me, and with a pointed finger, he acknowledged my presence. "Hey there, Mr. Hawthorne, right?" His smile seemed friendly enough, but there was a hint of suspicion in his eyes that threw me off. "You know who I am, sir?" I replied, my confusion evident.

"Yeah, your reputation precedes you," he answered, his tone genial. "Taking down crime rings and still keeping Everhaven's spirit alive. Let's give it up for Mr. Hawthorne," he declared, prompting applause from the press.

Once the applause died down, I spoke again. "Thanks, sir, I appreciate the recognition. But, if I can be frank, Everhaven's facing some serious challenges right now. Ever since Mayor Fairweather passed away, crime's through the roof, and religious tensions are at an all-time high. The peace we've always known is slipping away. How do you plan on bringing back that sense of safety and security to our city?"

"Thank you for your concern, Mr. Hawthorne, and for highlighting the challenges Everhaven currently faces. Rest assured, ensuring the safety and well-being of our citizens is my top priority. We recognize the gravity of the situation, especially with the recent increase in crime and tensions. Rebuilding the peace and security of Everhaven will require collaboration and dedication from all members of our community. Together, we will work tirelessly to restore our city to its rightful place as a beacon of safety, unity, and prosperity." Caidwall stated. Caidwall then proceeded to say "Alright, that's enough for today, have an amazing day!" he said with an enthusiastic voice. Though he told me how he knew me, I couldn't shake the feeling that things were about to get much weirder.

I started walking away back to my office, Ronnie caught up behind me, "Alex, he recognized you. Good stuff." Ronnie said as he slapped my back in support, he then noticed my distracted look, "What's up? You're good?" he said. I shook it off and replied "Yeah, just an odd feeling." I said. Ronnie may have been my boss but he was also a best friend since I was hired at the Everhaven Chronicles, I thought I could trust him with everything...

He then looked at me and instantly knew what I was talking about, "Hey Caidwall is going to be a great mayor." he exclaimed, I looked at him and felt a little nervousness in my heart, "I've been thinking about Caidwall. It's weird how as soon as Fairweather was out of the picture, Caidwall came in."

Ronnie immediately started acting nervous and annoyed, "I-, wha- What are you trying to say?" he said. I replied with, "Ronnie, I don't know, I'm just tired. I'mma go to the office, pick up a couple of things and head home." Ronnie immediately calmed down. "O- Ok." he said as he adjusted his shirt.

20 minutes passed and I arrived at my office, I entered and packed my phone, my wallet, my keys, and the rest of my belongings. As I held my bag and proceeded to the door, my office phone started ringing. It was late so I had no idea who it could be. I walked over and picked up the phone, "Alex Hawthorne, how may I-." The voice cut me off, "Hawthorne, Caidwall is not who you think he is, investigate the death of

Eris Stoneheart!" The voice was rushed and deep, "Look buddy, it's late, and the caffeine is starting to wear off. So how about you shut the fuck up and go to sle-." He cut me off again, "Unless you want Everhaven to be dust, Investigate!" The voice hung up the phone. Stoneheart... the name was familiar to me, it was the surname of the reporter that asked Caidwall about gas emissions. I thought nothing of it and headed home. On my drive home, I thought of this Eris Stoneheart and how she connected to the other Evelyn Stoneheart. However, I shrugged it off and thought it was a prank call, then I arrived home.

I opened my door, "Jason!" I yelled, "I'm home!"

Let me reintroduce myself, I'm Alex Hawthorne, I'm 34 years old and I have a 16 year old son, Jason. When I was 24, my wife, Aliah Hawthorne fell victim to organized crime. Since that day I've devoted my life to protecting my son more, and becoming a journalist to make sure another crime befalls someone ever again.

Jason started running down the stairs, "Hey Dad." Jason saw the confused look in my eye, "What's wrong?" I assured him, "Oh? Nothing, got a prank call today. These fuckin' internet trolls think they're funny."

He started laughing,"Ha! Anyways, I'm going to my room to do homework. Good night." He said as he ran to give me a hug. I gave him a kiss on the head and said "Good Night." He ran to his room.

I trudged up the stairs, bypassing Jason's room with a heavy heart. Sitting down at my laptop in my own room, I couldn't shake the nagging doubts that clouded my mind.

Caidwall's promises echoed in my thoughts, taunting me with the allure of safety and security. But deep down, I knew better than to trust somebody like that right away. My wife, bless her soul, had learned that lesson the hard way.

I couldn't help but think back to the day she died, lured into a trap by promises of a big story. She was a journalist, like me, and she had dedicated her life to exposing corruption in Everhaven. But her bravery had cost her everything.

Mugsy Throught, the notorious gangster from Everhaven's dark past, had set her up, using her investigations into Mayor Cade's shady dealings as bait. It was a bitter reminder of the dangers lurking in the shadows of our city.

As I sat there, lost in thought, I couldn't shake the feeling that she would have wanted me to continue her work. Despite the risks, despite the uncertainty, I owed it to her to carry on the fight against corruption.

So, with a heavy sigh and a sense of determination burning in my chest, I made a decision. My curiosity may have gotten the best of me, but I couldn't let fear dictate my actions. After all, what's life without a little adventure, right?

I decided to do a quick online search about Eris Stoneheart. Surprisingly, there was little information available, but it mentioned she was a reporter. Curiosity gnawed at me, and I couldn't shake off the urgency in the mysterious caller's voice. With a sigh, I decided to dig deeper into the connection between Eris, Caidwall, and Evelyn Stoneheart. Little did I know, this seemingly random call would unravel a web of secrets and mysteries in the year to come...

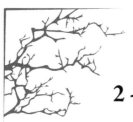

2 - Stoneheart

After a couple of days of digging into Eris Stoneheart's background, I stumbled upon something unsettling: she had passed away just weeks before the election, apparently from a heart attack. "A heart attack?" I muttered to myself, skepticism gnawing at me as I sat behind my laptop. "We'll see about that."

As I dug deeper into the rabbit hole of mystery surrounding Eris Stoneheart's demise, I couldn't shake the feeling that I was onto something big. Or maybe it was just the pizza I had for lunch. Either way, Evelyn Stoneheart seemed like a key piece of the puzzle, and I was determined to unlock the truth, even if it meant facing more questions than answers. I had also seen that Evelyn's office, "The Everhaven Times" didn't exist.

With a mix of determination and curiosity fueling my every step, I marched toward the Stoneheart residence like a detective on a mission. Well, more like a detective with a slight limp from sitting at my desk for too long. But you get the idea.

As I approached their front door, I couldn't help but wonder what kind of mysteries awaited me on the other side. Would Evelyn be a helpful ally in my quest for answers, or would she turn out to be the mysterious caller leading me on a wild goose chase? Only one way to find out, I supposed. Time to knock on the door and hope for the best.

Upon reaching the Stoneheart residence, I took a deep breath and rang the doorbell. Moments later, the door creaked open, revealing a weary-looking woman who bore a striking resemblance to Eris. "Can I help you?" she asked, her voice tinged with curiosity.

"I'm sorry to bother you," I began, struggling to find the right words. "I'm investigating some... inconsistencies regarding Eris Stoneheart's passing, and I was hoping to speak with someone who knew her well."

The woman's expression shifted, a flicker of concern crossing her features. "I'm Evelyn, Eris's sister," she said softly. "Please, come in."

As we sat down in the cozy living room, Evelyn's eyes searched mine, as if trying to gauge my intentions. "What exactly do you want to know?" she inquired, her tone cautious yet inviting.

Taking a moment to gather my thoughts, I explained "I just need to understand what happened to Eris, judges wrote her death off as a heart attack. However, I think there's more to the case." I confessed, my voice filled with a mixture of determination and desperation.

In that moment, as I glanced at Evelyn, her eyes met mine with a flicker of recognition. "Wait a minute," she said, her voice trailing off as realization dawned. "I remember you... from Caidwall's speech."

My heart skipped a beat. "Yes, that's right," I replied, caught off guard by her recognition. "I remember seeing you there too."

Instantly, Evelyn sprang into action, her movements frantic as she darted around the room like a cat chasing a laser pointer. "What the hell?" I exclaimed, caught off guard by her sudden urgency. She hurried to the windows, pulling the curtains shut with a determined flick of her wrist.

I trailed after her, trying to make sense of the chaos unfolding before me. When she reached the kitchen, retrieved a gun from one of the drawers, and pointed it at me, I couldn't help but raise an eyebrow. "Whoa, whoa. Cool it, peanut," I quipped, trying to lighten the mood as I raised my hands in mock surrender.

But Evelyn was dead serious, her gaze steely as she leveled the gun in my direction. "Back on the sofa. Now!" she commanded, her tone leaving no room for argument. Reluctantly, I complied, sinking back onto the cushions with a sense of unease settling over me.

"Whoa, whoa, easy there! You're pointing that thing at me like it's a TV remote and I'm the volume button. Let's take a deep breath and talk this out over a cup of coffee, or maybe a dinner date-" She interrupted me, "Shut up! Who sent you? It was that asshole, Caidwall, wasn't it?" She frantically said. My confusion got the better of me, "Wha- I-, what the fuck are you talking about?!" I exclaimed, "I don't know wha-" She interrupted me once more,

"DON'T LIE TO ME!" she yelled as she rushed to press the barrel of the pistol against my head, "OKAY, OKAY! SOMEBODY CALLED ME SAYING TO INVESTIGATE YOUR SISTER'S DEATH AND THAT IF I DIDN'T THAT EVERHAVEN WOULD BE DUST!" I yelled as I covered my head.

Evelyn pulled the gun back, her confusion evident. She then ran back up the stairs, As Evelyn dashed up the stairs, leaving me stranded in the dimly lit foyer, my heart went into full sprint mode. Seriously, it felt like it was training for a marathon.

Taking a moment to catch my breath, I couldn't help but wonder: why was Evelyn so aggressive? Why did she mention Caidwall? And who on earth thought it was a good idea to dial my number and drop this fucking mystery in my lap?

I shook my head, feeling like I'd stumbled into a bad detective novel, but hey, at least I wasn't the one holding the gun, right? Silver linings, and all that jazz. I decided that it was time to channel my inner Sherlock and figure this shit out.

I got my shit together and stood up, I proceeded up the stairs. I saw Evelyn speaking to herself, packing her stuff with her gun still tight in her hands. "Not safe anymore... fuckin' hell." she muttered. "We good now?" I exclaimed, she shut her suitcase and placed her gun in her pants. She pushed into me and walked down the stairs. I followed her down the staircase, "Wha-?" I muttered to myself.

"You're not safe here either. I suggest you get out of here," Evelyn said coolly as she headed for the door. I scrambled to follow her, grabbing her arm in desperation. "No way! You've gotta spill the beans on what the hell is going on!" I demanded, my heart racing a mile a minute.

Before she could reply, a sudden flash of light caught my eye. I turned to see headlights approaching fast from the left. Gripping Evelyn's arm tighter, I braced myself for whatever was about to go down.

As the car screeched to a halt, two guys in suits hopped out, looking as shady as a back alley at midnight. "Can we help you?" Evelyn called out, her voice dripping with sarcasm.

But before we could even blink, the two guys whipped out tommy guns like something straight out of a gangster movie. Bullets started flying, and Evelyn and I made a mad dash for cover behind her car.

"Shit, shit, shit!" I muttered under my breath as I dodged the hail of gunfire, my heart pounding like a jackhammer. Evelyn yelled for me to follow her, and I didn't need to be told twice. With a final curse, I dove into the passenger seat, barely escaping the bullets whizzing past.

Evelyn revved the engine like she was auditioning for a Fast and Furious movie, and we peeled out of there like bats out of hell. My heart was pounding at this point, I couldn't breathe. Evelyn noticed this as she was driving, "What happened?!" She exclaimed, my heart was pounding and I couldn't mutter any words, "Wa- Water." I softly said, struggling to speak. She grabbed water from the back and gave it to me. I took it and hey let me tell you, that was the best fuckin' sip i've ever taken.

I calmed down with every sip, "I'm getting too old for this." I said as I put down the water, Evelyn started softly laughing. Enraged, I looked at her and laid it down on her, "You can't be laughing right now! Tell me why I get a call saying to investigate *your* sister's death, then when I do first *you* pull a gun, then Bonnie and Clyde back there pull guns on me. What the fuck is going on?!" I yelled. "I did some digging, the people you work for: The Everhaven Times, they don't exist. Who... are... you?"

"Relax, I'll explain soon. We're almost there."

As Evelyn's words hung in the air, I couldn't help but feel a knot of anxiety tightening in my stomach. "Almost where?" I pressed, my voice edged with frustration and fear.

But Evelyn remained tight-lipped, her focus fixed on the road ahead. With each passing mile, the tension in the car seemed to mount, like we were hurtling towards an uncertain fate with no way to steer clear.

As we rounded a bend in the road, Evelyn finally broke her silence. "We're going to a safe place," she said cryptically, her tone laced with a hint of urgency. I furrowed my brow, trying to make sense of her vague explanation. "A safe place?" I repeated, my mind racing with possibilities. "What, are we going to a secret bunker or something? Do I need to start stocking up on fuckin' canned goods and conspiracy theories?"

But before Evelyn could respond, exhaustion washed over me like a tidal wave, and my eyelids grew heavy. Despite my best efforts to stay awake, sleep claimed me, leaving Evelyn to navigate the winding road ahead alone.

And as I drifted into unconsciousness, I couldn't help but imagine what I was going to do next. Maybe we'd stumble upon a gang of time-traveling aliens or a troop of tap-dancing penguins. Either way, I was in for one hell of a nap.

3 - Everhaven Times

"Wakey wakey, rise and shine!" Evelyn's voice jolted me awake, and I groaned, feeling like I'd been hit by a truck. I squinted against the blinding sunlight streaming through the car window, wondering why morning felt like it had just sucker-punched me. I saw that we were at an apartment building back in good ol' Everhaven.

"Where are we?" I asked, my heart racing with a mixture of confusion and embarrassment at having conked out like a lightbulb.

Evelyn shot me a look that was halfway between amusement and exasperation. "Welcome to your new digs, Sleeping Beauty," she teased, her tone playful but with a hint of seriousness underlying it.

My jaw practically hit the floor. "Wait, what? You're telling me I got shot at last night, and now I'm crashing at some random apartment building?" I exclaimed, trying to inject some humor into the situation to mask my disbelief. However, Evelyn's expression remained more serious. "Hey, don't knock it till you've tried it. Besides, it's better than sleeping in the car, right?"

I had to admit, she had a point. With a resigned sigh, I unbuckled my seatbelt and followed Evelyn out of the car, bracing myself for whatever insanity awaited us behind the doors of our new temporary abode. As I walked out of the car, I remembered something... Jason, he didn't know where I was, I frantically checked for my pockets, "Ah fuck!" I yelled. Evelyn quickly turned around confused, "What?" she exclaimed.

"My phone was in my car!" I exclaimed, frustrated. "I have to call my son."

Evelyn without any doubt in her eyes gave me her small cell phone right away. "Hurry, we gotta get inside." she said. I frantically took the phone and rushed to dial my son's number. The number was ringing, "Come on, come on." I said hoping that Jason was okay and well. Then suddenly, the phone picked up, "Hello? Dad?" said Jason. "Thank god, are you okay Jason?" I exclaimed, happy to hear his voice. "Dad..." Jason spoke softly,

"What? Jason?" I said confused on the softness of his voice, "Dad, please help m-"

I heard shuffling in the phone, like somebody was snatching his phone from him, "Jason!" I yelled. Then, somebody else came on the phone, "Hey, Jason isn't here right now. Could I take a message?" The man said with a deep voice. "I'm going to strangle you alive! Where's my son?!" I said.

"Hey don't worry, we're all chilling right now. All 3 of us. Nothing is going to happen to him as long as you follow our instructions." The man said. I got furious, "If you lay a finger on him, I'm going to take your arms and shove it up your ass!" I said. "All we need is Miss Stoneheart, and your son is free." he exclaimed, "We'll be in touch."

The man hanged up, I was in a state of shock. This case that dropped into my lap had gotten my son captured, and it was all my fault. I gave Evelyn her phone back and then our eyes caught each other. They both locked, "Whatever you did got my son captured. Who are you and what is going on?!" I yelled out.

She sighed, "I'm sorry, come with me. I'll explain everything."

After 20 minutes of trudging through that creepy abandoned apartment, we finally entered a room. I'll admit, I was expecting a total dump, but when I stepped inside, it was like walking into a tech-savvy nerd's paradise. There were computers everywhere, and 2 people hunched over them like they were on a mission from the nerd gods.

As soon as we walked in, they all turned to look at us, and Evelyn made introductions like we were VIPs crashing a nerd convention. "Guys, this is Mr. Hawthorne," she said, gesturing towards me like I was some kind of celebrity.

I took a step back, feeling a little awkward under their gaze, but to my surprise, they started clapping. "Uh, hi?" I said, totally confused as to why they were applauding me. I mean, I hadn't even done anything yet.

However, Evelyn seemed to think it was all perfectly normal. "Mr. Hawthorne, they're big fans of yours. They've been following your paper since Mayor Fairweather got elected," she explained, like I was some kind of local hero or something.

I couldn't help but chuckle at the absurdity of it all. Here I was, expecting to stumble upon some shady underground operation, and instead, I was getting a standing ovation from a bunch of tech geeks. Life sure had a funny way of surprising the shit out of you.

The young woman in her teens spoke up, "I'm Crissy, thank you for everything you do for Everhaven Alex- I mean- Mr.-

Hawthorne- sir." she said completely geeked out. "Thanks, you can call me Alex. I don't really care for formalities." I said, mildly smiling at her excitement.

I looked over to the man with glasses in his mid 20s. "And you? What's your name son?' I asked. He fixed his posture on the chair and spoke up as well, "I'm Jacob. Evelyn, why is Mr. Hawthorne here?" he said, maintaining his stature.

"Yeah, Stoneheart, you still haven't answered my question." I said as I turned to Evelyn, she sat down and began to explain. "Again, I'm very sorry about your son but..."

She started from the beginning, "My sister, Eris Stoneheart, she was quite the reporter. She worked for The Everhaven Chronicles. Just before the election, she stumbled upon something big. It was about this guy running for mayor, Richard Caidwall. Eris received a leak from an anonymous source, revealing that Caidwall was allegedly greasing the palms of the Throught gang to destroy low income homes to build more offices to secure his path to mayorship." she said, I could see in her eyes her care for her sister. However, I quickly realized she was working at the same office as me yet I never noticed her. "She then went to follow up on a lead and..." Evelyn began tearing up, "She died trying to protect me and our home. Judges and your Everhaven Chronicles ruled it off as an 'heart attack'."

She stood up again, "I *know* it was Caidwall, and ever since I've been trying to find leads to try to expose him for the evil fuckin' dickhead that he is."

"We *all* are." Crissy added.

Everything around me just froze for a beat. All those suspicions I had about Caidwall suddenly seemed to align. I couldn't shake the thought of Mayor Fairweather's demise possibly being linked to him. And then, the worst fear crept in – what if my son was next on his list?

I glanced back up at Evelyn, trying to keep cool, "Why not just tell this to a proper news outlet? They'd have to sniff around if there's a lead like this." But Evelyn's reaction was fiery, to say the least. "I wish it were that simple! Caidwall's got half the newsrooms in his pocket, and even your beloved Everhaven Chronicles isn't immune," she spat out.

That's when it clicked. Ronnie... Nah, he couldn't have been bought out, right? But then I remembered how twitchy he got when Caidwall's name came up in conversation about Fairweather's death. "No, not Ronnie," I mumbled to myself, trying to dispel the thought. With a determined nod, I turned to leave.

"Where are you off to?" Jacob blurted out.

"I'm off to do some digging. I'll be back before you know it," I declared, ready to unravel the mysteries of this city and try to rescue my boy, Jason. "I'm coming with you!" Evelyn exclaimed, "I don't know who called you about my sister but I do know that it's my fault that you and your son are in this situation." She said as she caught up with me. I couldn't help but softly smile.

After another twenty minutes of exiting the building, me and Evelyn entered her car, "Where to?" she asked as she turned to me.

I started thinking for a minute, "786 Faircreek Drive. Mayor Fairweather's home, we're going to get some answers." I firmly said.

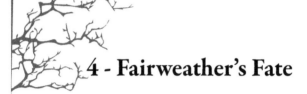

4 - Fairweather's Fate

P icture this: a moon so bright it could practically guide you to your next clue, and here we are, Evelyn Stoneheart and yours truly, Alex Hawthorne, embarking on our very own Nancy Drew adventure. Well, if Nancy Drew had a knack for cracking cases instead of just solving mysteries.

The air was thick with anticipation as we approached the towering mansion of Mayor Fairweather. You could practically taste the intrigue in the air, or maybe that was just the lingering scent of Evelyn's determination mixed with a hint of my own nerves.

Evelyn's flashlight beam cut through the darkness like a hot knife through butter, revealing the path to potential answers. And let me tell you, those gates protested like they'd been waiting years to do so. I joked about needing a jungle machete instead of a notepad for this gig, but Evelyn's death stare quickly shut down my attempt at levity. Stepping into the old mayor's mansion felt like crashing a party where the guests were long gone, leaving behind only dust and secrets. The air was thick with history, and every creak of the floorboards seemed to whisper, "Welcome to the mystery zone."

With Evelyn leading the charge, we ventured deeper into the mansion, our senses on high alert like a pair of over caffeinated bloodhounds. I half-expected Mayor Fairweather himself to jump out from behind a curtain and spill the beans on his own demise. But alas, the only thing jumping out at us was the occasional moth.

"After Fairweather passed away, his wife moved. It's unfortunate innit?" Evelyn said as we walked up the huge staircase. I looked around and just felt down about how one of the city's best mayors might have been murdered. "Yeah." I mumbled.

We proceeded even further and arrived at Fairweather's quarters. It literally said 'Carter Fairweather' in bold letters on the door. "Wow, talk about stating the obvious! I guess subtlety isn't Fairweather's strong suit. Maybe he should consider a career in billboard advertising instead of mayor." Evelyn jokingly exclaimed as she entered the room. I followed behind, "Hey, careful who you're talking about. Since Fairweather got elected, gangs like the Throught gang have been more on the down low." I said, reminding her how impactful Fairweather was as a mayor.

We entered and saw complete dustiness, "This shit smells like the fuckin' doctor's office." I jokingly said as I covered my nose to protect myself from the horrible smell. No but for real, it smelled like three dozen rats died there. Don't ask me how I know what that smells like.

As we searched around the room, me and Evelyn made conversation, "Alex, you grew up around here?" she said as she searched around the bed, "Yep, good ol' Everhaven. Married the love of my life too but she's gone now unfortunately." I sadfully said as I searched the closet. She called for my attention, "I'm sorry for your loss. It's just you and Jason?" she asked with care in her tone.

"Yeah, that's exactly why I can't lose him, Evelyn. He's all I got." I said as I peered at her. "What about you, I mean what's the deal with Crissy and Jacob?" I asked.

"Jacob Clairegiven worked with Eris at the chronicles a while back, but after her death, he came to me wanting to help me. Crissy Stace though is the saddest. She was homeless before I found her, but I took her in, you know; gave her purpose." She said, smiling at the thought of both of them, "They're *my* family."

She then noticed something to my right, she walked over, "Wait, what's that?" she exclaimed as she reached for what seemed like a door handle. She opened the hidden door to find a secret work room.

To both our surprises, the room was completely in shambles with the light turned on. Documents and letters all over the floor. Somebody had been here recently, I quickly looked out the room trying to see if someone was possibly still in the building. "We need to hurry it up." I nervously said. She promptly agreed and we both began searching the work room, "These letters are from Caidwall to Fairweather. Caidwall was trying to bribe Fairweather into stepping down as mayor." Evelyn said as she read off of one of the letters.

I picked up another letter and began reading off of it, "Looks like Fairweather denied bribe money, and Caidwall started threatening him. Then, Caidwall killed him..." I said as my face widened. I kept reading through the horrible handwriting. No really, Caidwall's handwriting was horrible for a supposed dirty criminal.

"It also looks like Fairweather cursed him off and Caidwall stopped writing," I stated. Evelyn continued to shuffle through the mess of papers, and she found one that stood out. "Whoa. This is a list of the news offices, courtrooms, and police stations on Caidwall's payroll. Woah Alex, he has ties to the White House." Evelyn said as she analyzed the graph. I got confused; why would Fairweather have a list of that?

I took the paper from her hand, hoping that my office wouldn't be there. I thoroughly searched, and... I saw it. The Everhaven Chronicles was under Caidwall's payroll. I felt betrayed and angry. How could Ronnie agree to all of this? And keep it from me?

Before I could voice my concerns, we heard a noise from outside the room. It sounded like glass shattering down the stairs. I gave Evelyn the paper, looked at her, and spoke in a low tone, "Stuff everything you can into your bag," I whispered as I began to go confront whoever was in the house. Before I left, Evelyn grabbed my arm. "Don't die," she softly exclaimed. I nodded and proceeded outside.

As I made my way towards the source of the disturbance, my heart was racing faster than a cheetah chasing its lunch. Every step felt like a countdown to a bombshell revelation, and I couldn't shake the feeling that something big was about to hit the fan.

But as I rounded the corner and peered down the stairs, my eyes widened in shock. There, amidst the shattered glass, stood Ronnie, looking like he'd been caught red-handed with his hand in the cookie jar. My jaw practically hit the floor as I struggled to comprehend what I was seeing.

"Ronnie? What the fuck are you doing here?!" I blurted out, my voice a mix of disbelief and fury. I could feel my blood boiling, my anger simmering just beneath the surface. Ronnie's eyes darted around nervously, like a deer caught in headlights. "Alex, listen, I can explain," he started, but I wasn't having any of it. "Explain? You're under Caidwall's payroll, Ronnie! How could you betray me like this?" I practically yelled, my words echoing off the walls of the mansion.

Before Ronnie could come up with some feeble excuse, Evelyn stepped in, her bag filled to the brim with the incriminating evidence that we had found. She looked at Ronnie in disappointment.

I could feel my hands shaking with rage as I tried to process the betrayal. It was like a punch to the gut, leaving me reeling and struggling to make sense of it all. But one thing was clear: the corruption in Everhaven ran deeper than I ever imagined, and Ronnie was right in the thick of it.

As the shock began to fade, it was quickly replaced by a seething anger that bubbled up from deep within me. How could Ronnie, someone I trusted like a brother, stoop so low? The realization hit me like a ton of bricks, leaving me feeling betrayed and utterly dumbfounded.

"Explain yourself, Ronnie. Now," I demanded, my voice trembling with a mixture of fury and hurt.

Ronnie's eyes darted around nervously, searching for words that could possibly justify his betrayal. But his silence spoke volumes, confirming my worst fears.

Evelyn's hand rested on my shoulder, her touch grounding me in the midst of my swirling emotions. "We need answers, The truth, no lies," she said, her voice firm and unwavering.

With a heavy sigh, Ronnie finally spoke, his voice barely above a whisper. "I got in over my head, okay? Caidwall... he had dirt on me, things I thought were buried in the past. I didn't have a choice, but his plan for the city *is* shaping up." he confessed, his words dripping with pride. But his excuses fell on deaf ears. The damage was done, and I couldn't bring myself to forgive him so easily. My fists clenched at my sides, the urge to lash out almost overwhelming.

As we stood there, stunned by the revelation of Ronnie's involvement, my anger began to simmer beneath the surface like a pot about to boil over.

But before I could process my emotions, Ronnie's eyes landed on Evelyn's bag, bulging with incriminating evidence. His expression darkened, and a tense silence settled over the room like a heavy fog.

"I can't let you leave with that," Ronnie said, his voice low and resolute.

Evelyn and I exchanged wary glances, unsure of what Ronnie was planning. The air crackled with tension as we stood there, each of us sizing up the others, unsure of what would happen next. "Why not? What are you going to do with it?" Evelyn asked, her voice steady despite the uncertainty hanging in the air. Ronnie's jaw clenched, and for a moment, it looked like he was about to snap. But then, his expression softened, and he let out a heavy sigh.

"I'm sorry, Alex. Ms. Stoneheart. But I can't let you walk away with those papers. Not while I still have a chance to set things right," Ronnie said, his tone tinged with firmness. I looked over at Evelyn, "Get the car ready, this won't take long." I said as I rolled up my sleeves.

I felt a surge of frustration and disappointment wash over me. Ronnie was supposed to be on our side, fighting alongside me to bring down any corruption plaguing our city. But now, it seemed like he was choosing a different path, one that led straight into the heart of darkness.

"You've always been blind and stupid, Alex." Ronnie said as he also geared up for the fight that was bound to happen. Before he could start his rant, I rushed towards him and threw a punch, but he dodged it. "Politics is a messy business. Sometimes, in order to get things done and make real change, you have to play the game. It's not pretty, but it's the reality of the situation!" Ronnie exclaimed as he charged into me, his attack pinned me at the wall. I punched him in the mouth, "I trusted you!" I yelled, "You were there, at my wedding! At my son's birth!" I stated as I punched him in the mouth again, sending him against a portrait.

"We were supposed to clean the city together!" I said as I threw another punch, this time he dodged the punch and kicked me in the stomach knocking me to the ground, gasping for breath, I struggled to my feet, the pain of betrayal gnawing at my insides like a relentless beast. Ronnie loomed over me, his expression a mix of anger and frustration.

"You think you're the hero here, Alex?" Ronnie's voice dripped with bitterness, each word like a dagger to my wounded heart. "Just like Aliah, always trying to play the savior. Look where that got her."

His words hit me like a tidal wave, dredging up memories I'd tried so hard to bury. The image of Aliah, my beloved wife, flashed before my eyes, her determination to expose corruption etched into my soul like a scar. I looked back up at him, "Don't talk about my *fucking* wife!" I screamed as I dashed up and socked him in the jaw, sending him to the ground on the brink of losing consciousness. I stood over Ronnie, feeling the betrayal in my stomach and I thought about how someone I thought as a brother, how bad he lost his way.

"You may have lost your way, Ronnie," I said, my voice tinged with sadness. "But I won't let you drag me down with you."

Suddenly, I couldn't breathe. My anxiety, fear, and adrenaline caught up to me and I fell over, I was trying to get back up and struggling to breathe at the same time. Then, I focused on my breathing, it got better and I got back up.

Ronnie also struggled to get up, his body battered and bruised, but he couldn't muster the strength. He looked at me, desperation and defiance burning in his eyes.

"You're blind, Alex!" Ronnie's voice was raw with pain, his words cutting through the tense silence. "The city's been in the gutter since Mayor Cade! Caidwall is offering us a chance at a better future, even if it's under his thumb. If you can't see that, then you're already a lost cause! You don't stand a chance against him! Caidwall's got everyone in his back pocket. You'll never be able to take him down."

His words stung like salt in a wound, but I refused to let them break me. With a roar of anger, I faced him head-on.

"You betrayed me, Ronnie, and that's all you have to say?!" I shouted, my fists clenched in frustration. "Tell Caidwall I'm coming for him, and I'm getting my son back too."

With that, I stormed out of the building, leaving Ronnie behind in a heap on the floor. Outside, Evelyn was waiting in the car, her expression a mix of concern and determination. I slid into the passenger seat, wiping the blood from my hands as I recounted the confrontation.

"Yeah, it went as smooth as a rollercoaster ride in an earthquake," I muttered, trying to lighten the mood. Evelyn inspected my hand, her brow furrowed with worry.

"Damn, looks like you've been through the wringer," she said, her tone tinged with concern. "But we've got work to do. Let's take down Caidwall and get your son back, once and for all."

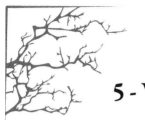

5 - Veils Lifted

2 weeks passed, we all worked together to find leads wherever we could. Eris's involvement with Caidwall, Caidwall bribing and killing fairweather, Caidwall buying out judges. All In print. As I worked together with Evelyn, Jacob, Crissy; I grew quite fond of them, I started seeing them more as a family. You know that weird fuzzy feeling that you get when you're around people you actually mess with? That times 5. After the 2 weeks were over, we put all of our evidence on the table.

I turned on the television, with the news playing, "Everhaven's peace has returned with the new mayor, Richard Caidwall. Will the citizens of this city finally have their peace?" The reporter stated. Evelyn came over, watching the report with me, "The people are scared." Evelyn said as she peered at me. I looked back at her, "They're not going to get peace, not from Caidwall." We then heard Crissy behind us.

"Okay, so how do we get these out?" Crissy said. Evelyn peered at Crissy, "I don't know, Caidwall would shut any attempt at this evidence getting run." she said, frustrated. "We need to release it ourselves but on a private network."

I looked over at Evelyn confused, "Why? Caidwall can't control the public network, whatever goes on the internet, will remain." I said. She explained, "Everhaven runs on a private network, so whatever goes on the internet is monitored by the mayor's office. If we post this, it's for sure going to get taken down." She stated as she stood up, "So we have to get on our own private network."

I thought for a minute, we had the evidence; why couldn't we just threaten Caidwall with it? "I have a plan." I stated, my voice overpowering the room, "I'm going to threaten Caidwall with the evidence, have him step down as mayor, and get my son back."

Evelyn peered at me in fear, "That's a bad idea!" She exclaimed trying to reason with me, "Caidwall is going to shut you up immediately!" She started tearing up, "I don't want what happened to Eris to happen to you."

I reassured Evelyn, placing a gentle hand on her shoulder. "Don't worry, Ev. I've faced tough situations before and come out on top. This won't be any different."

Jacob leaned in, his expression serious. "But Alex, getting to Caidwall won't be a walk in the park. It's risky." I nodded, acknowledging the gravity of the situation. "I know it won't be easy, but it's our best shot at either getting the evidence out safely or having him step down." Crissy chimed in, her voice determined. "We've got your back, Alex. Just let us know if you need anything."

Evelyn's concern was palpable as she caught up to me at the door, her grip tight on my arm. "Please, Alex, promise me you'll be careful. I've already lost Eris, I jus-," she pleaded, her eyes searching mine for reassurance, but I interrupted her.

"I promise. I'll do everything in my power to make it back in one piece." With that, I left the room, Evelyn's worried expression lingering in my mind as I prepared to face the challenges ahead. I looked back quickly, "I'll be back before you can say 'Caidwall's a slimy bitch' three times fast!" I jokingly exclaimed. "Uh Evelyn, I don't really got a ride so I'm taking your car!"

After what felt like an eternity, I finally parked in front of my house and stepped out of the car. My heart pounded in my chest as I approached the front door, each step heavy with dread. Going back into that chaos, it felt like walking into a nightmare I couldn't escape.

Entering the house, I was met with the sight of destruction. The living room was a damn huge mess, a painful reminder of the events that had unfolded there. With a heavy heart, I made my way upstairs, my footsteps echoing in the silence.

Jason's room was a fuckin' scene of devastation, his belongings strewn across the floor. But it was the sight of dried blood staining the carpet that made my blood run cold. Anger and fear surged within me as I clenched my fists, vowing to bring those responsible to justice. "Caidwall, when I get my hands on you..."

Descending the stairs, I headed for the home phone, my hands trembling as I dialed Jason's number. The ringing seemed to echo through the empty house, a haunting reminder of everything that had been lost.

But then, another sound cut through the silence – a ringing coming from upstairs. My heart skipped a beat as I hurried back up, my mind racing with fear and uncertainty.

As I reached the top of the stairs, the ringing grew louder, echoing off the walls like a sinister melody. My pulse quickened with each step, a knot of dread tightening in my stomach.

Pushing open the door to my bedroom, I followed the sound to its source. There, lying on the floor amidst the chaos, was Jason's old cell phone. Its screen illuminated with an incoming call, casting an eerie glow in the dim room.

As I reached for Jason's phone, confusion washed over me. How was it still here, untouched amidst the chaos? My mind raced with questions, but before I could make sense of it all, I heard a noise behind me.

As I turned around, I found myself face to face with one of the corrupt mayor's lackeys. He had that classic villain look down pat, with his fuckin' sinister grin and shifty eyes.

Before I could even muster a witty comeback, he swung at me with all the finesse of a bull in a china shop. The next thing I knew, I was seeing stars and doing an impromptu dance routine as I stumbled backwards. As I tried to regain my bearings, the room spun around me like a bad carnival ride. I must have looked like a drunk trying to walk a straight line.

Just when I thought things couldn't get any worse, I heard Mr. Thug's voice, dripping with all the charm of a sewer rat. "We knew you'd come sniffing around, Hawthorne," he jeered, his words laced with enough contempt to make even the toughest cookie crumble.

And with that, my world went as black as my coffee on a Monday morning. Talk about a knockout performance.

As I slowly shook off the haze of unconsciousness, I found myself in what seemed like a rejected set from a B-grade action movie. Dim lights, creepy warehouse vibes, and oh look, there's me, tied up like a fuckin' Thanksgiving turkey.

The two goons who put me in this predicament were standing there, looking like they just stepped out of a villain convention. The big one with the mean mug was doing his best impression of a Bond villain, while his scrawnier sidekick looked like he'd been practicing his evil laugh in front of a mirror.

"Well, well, well, look who decided to join the party," Mr. Mean Mug sneered, like he was auditioning for the role of Bad Guy #1 in a cheesy action flick.

His scrawny buddy, not to be outdone, chimed in with a smirk. "Yeah, you thought you could take on Mayor Caidwall? You're even dumber than you look."

I rolled my eyes, trying to play it cool despite the ropes digging into my wrists. "Hey, give me a fucking break. I've had worse Monday mornings," I quipped, because what's life without a little sarcasm. But deep down, I knew I had to find a way out of this shitstorm. After all, even the most hopeless situations can have a punchline – you just have to know where to look.

"Hey Mo! What you think we should do to this dumb muthafucka?" one of the goons sarcastically said to his partner, his dumbass lookin' partner replied with a smirk on his face, "Well Lar, I think we should cripple him for trying to mess up the mayor's image."

Lar chimed in, his tone dripping with sarcasm, "Oh yeah, Mo, that sounds like the best idea ever!" Before they could push me further, I interjected with a dramatic "Wait!" and blurted out, "Unless you want your super-secret operation to flop harder than a pancake on a hot griddle, I suggest we set up a little tête-à-tête with Mayor Backhand Benny himself." I flashed them a playful smirk.

The two exchanged skeptical glances. "You're bluffing," Lar shot back. I met his doubt with a grin as wide as the Grand Canyon. "Oh, Lar, my dear friend, between the incriminating evidence I found at Mayor Fairweather's place and the trail of bodies tied to ol' Backhand Benny, I assure you, I'm not bluffing." Sarcasm oozed from every word.

"Well, shit," Mo muttered, reaching for his phone. With a resigned sigh, he dialed what I assumed was Caidwall's number, and the call connected. Unfortunately, I couldn't make out much of the conversation over the sound of my own victory dance in my head.

As Mo hung up the phone, I couldn't resist a quippy remark. "Did master give you permission?" I joked, a smirk playing on my lips. But before I could savor the punchline, Mo started chuckling and punched me in the face. Everything went black.

When I finally regained consciousness, I found myself in an unexpected place: Mayor Caidwall's office. At first, the mayor greeted me with a veneer of kindness, all smiles and pleasantries. It was like being welcomed into the lion's den by a particularly charming lion.

But beneath the surface, I could sense the simmering undercurrent of danger. Mayor Caidwall's smile didn't quite reach his eyes, and there was a steely edge to his voice as he offered me a seat.

As I sat there, trying to gather my wits, I couldn't shake the feeling that I was in deep trouble. But hey, at least the decor was nice. Silver linings, right?

As Mayor Caidwall settled into his seat behind the imposing desk, his demeanor shifted subtly. The genial facade began to crack, revealing glimpses of the ruthless politician lurking beneath.

"So, Mr. Hawthorne, what brings you to my humble abode?" Mayor Caidwall inquired, his tone honeyed yet tinged with a hint of menace.

I squared my shoulders, trying to maintain a façade of confidence despite the knot of unease in my stomach. "Ah you know, just thought I'd drop by for a friendly chat," I sarcastically replied with a forced nonchalance, mentally kicking myself for the lame attempt at deflection.

Mayor Caidwall's lips curled into a knowing smirk, his eyes gleaming with a predatory glint. "Ah, of course, how could I forget our little tête-à-tête? It's not every day that a nosy journalist comes knocking on my door," he remarked, his tone dripping with sarcasm.

I braced myself for the inevitable confrontation, knowing that I was treading on dangerous ground. But as Mayor Caidwall leaned back in his chair, steepling his fingers with a sinister grin, I realized that I was about to face the biggest challenge of my career. And this time, there would be no witty one-liners or clever quips to save me.

Mayor Caidwall steepled his fingers with a sinister grin, the gravity of the situation settled heavily upon me. I could practically feel the weight of his gaze bearing down on me, like a predator sizing up its prey.

"So, Mr. Hawthorne, let's cut straight to the chase," Mayor Caidwall began, his voice smooth as silk but with a razor-sharp edge. "You've been poking your nose where it doesn't belong, stirring up trouble for me and my administration."

I swallowed hard, trying to muster up a shred of bravado in the face of his intimidating presence. "Just doing my job, Mayor," I replied, attempting to keep my voice steady despite the nerves.

Mayor Caidwall's smile widened, but there was no warmth in it, only thinly veiled contempt. "Ah, yes, the noble pursuit of truth and justice," he scoffed. "But let me make one thing perfectly clear, Mr. Hawthorne: in Everhaven, I am the law. And anyone who dares to challenge me will suffer the consequences."

As his words hung in the air like a dark cloud, I couldn't help but wonder if I'd bitten off more than I could chew. But as Mayor Caidwall leaned forward, his eyes boring into mine with unwavering intensity, I knew one thing for certain: I wasn't about to back down without a fight.

As Mayor Caidwall reclined in his chair, that smug smirk plastered on his face, he couldn't resist taking a jab. "You're a real piece of work, Hawthorne, you remind me of my son." he sneered, his voice oozing with contempt. "Everhaven needs order, security. And if that means throwing a few folks under the bus, well, that's just the cost of doing business."

I felt my blood boil at his arrogance. "You talk a big game, Mayor, but we both know you're just a two-bit thug in a fancy suit," I retorted, my voice laced with sarcasm. "Everhaven deserves better than your brand of 'leadership.'"

For a split second, Mayor Caidwall's facade cracked, revealing a glimpse of annoyance beneath the surface. But then, with a smug chuckle, he leaned in closer, his eyes boring into mine like daggers. "Ah, but Mr. Hawthorne, you underestimate the power of conviction," he purred, his tone dripping with menace. "In this game, the toughest decisions require nerves of steel."

His words hung in the air like a bad smell, a reminder of the uphill battle ahead. But I refused to back down. With a steely glare of my own, I knew I had to take down Mayor Caidwall and get Jason back, even if it meant going toe-to-toe with the devil himself.

A smug grin plastered on his face, I couldn't help but let out a chuckle. "You're a real piece of work too, Caidwall," I quipped, my voice laced with sarcasm. "I've met used car salesmen with more integrity than you."

Caidwall's smirk faltered for a moment, his eyes narrowing in annoyance. "Ah, the righteous journalist, always with the moral high ground," he retorted, his tone dripping with disdain. "But let's be real here, Hawthorne. You're just as much a part of this circus as I am."

I shrugged, refusing to let his words get to me. "Maybe so, but at least I'm not the one moonlighting as a mafia boss on the side," I shot back, a smirk playing on my lips.

Caidwall's expression darkened, his eyes flashing with anger. "You're playing a dangerous game, Hawthorne," he growled, his voice low and menacing. "In Everhaven, the tough decisions require guts. And you, my friend, are fresh out."

I couldn't help but laugh at his theatrics. "Gee, thanks for the pep talk, Mayor," I replied, my tone dripping with sarcasm. "But if you think I'm backing down now, you've got another thing coming."

Caidwall's smirk turned into a malicious grin as he reached for something beneath his desk. "You think you're so clever, don't you?" he sneered, his fingers curling around a small device. "But let me show you something, Hawthorne."

As Caidwall activated a device, a live video feed popped up, revealing a scene straight out of a nightmare. My stomach churned as I saw my son, Jason, being held hostage by one of Caidwall's goons, a gun menacingly pointed at his head.

As Caidwall's grin widened, a sense of dread settled over me like a heavy blanket. "Well, well, well, look what we have here, Hawthorne," he sneered, his voice dripping with malice. "Seems like your threats just hit a little snag."

My fists clenched at my sides, the urge to lunge at him almost overwhelming. "Let him go, Caidwall," I growled, trying my best to sound tough despite the knot of fear tightening in my chest. "This is between you and me."

Caidwall's chuckle sent a shiver down my spine, his dark amusement chilling me to the bone. "Oh, don't worry, Hawthorne," he replied, his tone dripping with sarcasm. "I'll let him go... once you've learned your lesson."

As I watched helplessly, a wave of panic washed over me. I couldn't lose Jason, not like this. He was all I had left.

"Do it!" Caidwall commanded his henchman, his voice cold and commanding. I felt my heart drop as the gun was pressed against Jason's blindfolded head, his screams echoing in my ears. "Stop!" I yelled, desperation creeping into my voice.

Caidwall's eyes bore into mine, his gaze unwavering. "Mr. Hawthorne, I'll let your son go on two conditions," he stated proudly. "Drop this case, as it's not going to work out for you... And give us Ms. Stoneheart and her little crew's operations base."

My mind raced as I weighed my options. I thought of Evelyn, Jacob, and Crissy, and the bond we had formed in our fight against this stupid asshole in the last couple of weeks. Betraying them was out of the question.

"No!" I exclaimed, my voice trembling with defiance. "I can't."

Caidwall's expression darkened, his patience wearing thin. "Do it!" he shouted, the threat implicit as the gun remained pressed against my son's temple. Fear and confusion clouded my thoughts, leaving me paralyzed with indecision.

As Caidwall's demands echoed in the tense silence, a heavy weight settled in the pit of my stomach. Betraying Evelyn, Jacob, and Crissy was a bitter pill to swallow, but the thought of losing Jason was unbearable.

With a heavy heart, I made my decision. "Fine," I said, my voice barely above a whisper. "I'll do it."

Caidwall's grin widened triumphantly, his satisfaction evident in every line of his face. "Good choice, Hawthorne," he said, his tone dripping with smugness. "Now, tell me where to find them."

I hesitated for a moment, the guilt gnawing at my insides. But in the end, it felt like the safety of my son outweighed everything else. "They're based in the old apartment on East End Street," I replied, my voice hollow with regret.

As I watched Caidwall relay the information to his men, a wave of anguish washed over me. I had betrayed my friends, compromised everything we had fought for. But as Jason's safety hung in the balance, I knew that I would do whatever it took to protect him, even if it meant sacrificing everything else.

And as I left Caidwall's office, the weight of my decision bore down on me like a ton of bricks. I felt sick to my stomach, consumed by guilt and self-loathing. How could I have betrayed the people who had stood by me, who had become like family to me?

I couldn't shake the feeling of betrayal, the knowledge that I had sold out my friends for the sake of my own son.

As I stumbled out of Caidwall's office, consumed by guilt and regret, a car pulled up to the curb with a screech of tires. My heart skipped a beat as one of Caidwall's men stepped out, Jason in tow.

Relief flooded through me as I rushed forward to embrace my son. Jason ran into my arms, his face pale and drawn with pain. "Dad, I'm so sorry," he whispered, tears welling up in his eyes. "I tried to fight them off, but they shot me in the foot."

My heart ached at the sight of Jason's injured foot, anger bubbling up inside me at the thought of what he had endured. But as I held him close, I knew that nothing else mattered in that moment except comforting my son.

"It's okay, Jason," I murmured, my voice choked with emotion. "You're safe now. That's all that matters."

As we made our way back home, Jason's arm draped over my shoulder for support. I couldn't shake the heavy weight of guilt that hung over me like a dark cloud.

Stepping through the door, the sight of the mess left behind by Caidwall's thugs hit me like a ton of bricks. It was a stark reminder of the chaos that had infiltrated our lives.

Together, Jason and I worked in silence to clean up the aftermath, each movement a painful reminder of the events that had unfolded. The silence between us was deafening, filled with unspoken words and shared grief.

Among the broken trinkets was an Islamic painting saying "Allah" . I was brought up in a Muslim household. Seeing the trinket reminded me of the life I had before Everhaven, a life of peace and happiness, where I didn't betray anyone.

Once the last speck of dirt was swept away, we collapsed onto the couch in exhaustion. Jason's eyes bore into mine, silently pleading for answers.

Taking a deep breath, I explained the gravity of the situation to him. "What happened today stays between us, Jason," I said, my voice grave. "We can't risk anyone finding out, or Caidwall will come for us."

Jason nodded solemnly, understanding the severity of the situation. "I won't say a word, Dad," he promised, his voice barely above a whisper.

Turning on the TV in search of distraction, my heart sank as the headline flashed across the screen: "Criminal Hacker Group Gets Taken Down." It felt like a punch to the gut, seeing my friends' faces plastered on the screen.

Guilt gnawed at me like a relentless beast as I watched their arrest unfold. In that moment, I realized the full extent of the consequences of my actions, and it weighed heavily on my conscience.

How could I do this? Stoop this fuckin' low?

6 - Those Who Believe

In that dim, worn-out bar, regret stuck to me like gum on a summer sidewalk. It had been a year since I pulled the dumbest move of my life, betraying my friends just to get Jason back.

Staring at myself in the dingy mirror in the bar, I looked like I'd aged a decade. Trying to be a hero for my kid turned out to be a crash course in loneliness and heartache.

Our house, once buzzing with laughter and video game battles, felt like a library with too many overdue fines. The look in my son's eyes wasn't just disappointment; it was a silent "You really messed up, Dad" that hit harder than any punchline.

Nights became a sad solo act, with me and a bottle of whatever numbed the pain. The warmth inside wasn't comforting; it was just a desperate attempt to fill the hole left by my own stupid choices.

Days blurred together, and my son became this distant figure in my life. Our talks sounded more like missed connections than the easy banter we used to have.

In the quiet moments, when the only noise was the hum of the refrigerator and my neighbor's dog barking at who knows what, the weight of what I did sank in. I bet everything on a lousy hand, and now I was stuck living with the consequences.

Time was supposed to patch things up, but the scars from that bonehead move still ached. I was just a guy stumbling through a world that looked a whole lot grayer when you've let down the one person who should always be in your corner.

I sat in the bar, wallowing in my own self pity; like usual. I thought about how there could have been a better option. One that saved Jason, Evelyn, Crissy, and Jacob; I also thought about Crissy and how I left a teenager, a kid Jason's age to be taken like that. However, before I could feel bad, I took a shot and the whiskey bottle quickly numbed my guilt again.

The bartender, a grizzled soul who'd probably seen more than his fair share of personal tragedies, chimed in with a wry smile, "You know, Alex, you're keeping me in service with your regular visits, but I'm starting to think you're training for a heavyweight drinking championship."

I chuckled, a bitter laughter that carried the weight of truth. "Well, someone's got to keep the lights on in this joint, right?"

He poured another glass, sliding it my way with a knowing look. "Lights are on, but it looks like nobody's home in that head of yours. What's eating at you, man?"

I hesitated for a moment, contemplating whether to spill my guts to the bartender. But the words spilled out anyway, like a confession I couldn't keep locked away. "I messed up, Joe. Big time. Betrayed my friends, lost touch with my kid, and now drowning my sorrows in this bottomless pit of regret."

Joe raised an eyebrow, pouring himself a shot as if to brace for the heavy conversation ahead. "Life's full of screw-ups, Alex. But sitting here, drowning your sorrows, won't fix a damn thing."

I nodded, the weight of his words sinking in. "I know, Joe. I just... I thought I was doing the right thing, you know? Getting my son back, protecting him. Now, I feel like I've ruined everything."

Joe leaned in, his gruff voice softened. "Listen, we're all flawed, Alex. The mayor didn't leave you with much of an option. Nevertheless, It's how you deal with the mess you made that matters. Maybe it's time to sober up, face the wreckage, and start rebuilding. Your kid might surprise you if you give him a chance."

He gestured at the empty glasses between us. "Or, you know, we can keep playing this game until we both forget what day it is."

I downed the last of my drink, frustration bubbling beneath the surface. "Yeah, well, I'm not exactly in the running for 'Father of the Year.' I've messed up too much, Joe. I'm beyond surprise; I'm practically a lost cause."

Pushing my stool back with a screech, I stumbled to my feet, the room spinning in sync with the whirlwind of emotions. "Thanks for the pep talk, Joe. But I've got a date with the shadows tonight. They seem to be the only ones who can stand me."

I left the bar in a haze of frustration and intoxication, the city lights now a chaotic blur. Maybe Joe was right, but the weight of regret still felt too heavy for me to bear. As the door closed behind me, I walked into the night, feeling like a ship lost in a stormy sea, unsure of the destination but certain of the turmoil within. During my walk, I sobered up a little and started walking home.

I walked home and I thought about what Joe had said; though his words came from a place of care, at the time, I felt like there wasn't anything that I could do to win back over my son and feel better for what I'd done.

Finally, I arrived at my house; I stumbled on my way inside. I opened the door, "Jas-onnn I'm homeee!" I exclaimed, my words slurring as I proceeded to lay down on the couch.

Jason came running down the stairs, he just turned 17 years old 2 weeks earlier. "Hey dad." Jason said with a smile, but his smile quickly turned into a frown when he saw my state of drunkenness. "Really, dad?" He said, frustrated and annoyed, "Again?"

"I've just been stressing lately, don't worry!" I happily exclaimed.

Jason peered at me, "You can't drink your way out of stress all the time." He said, anger fussing out of his words.

I tried to reassure Jason, "When you're older, you'll underst-" He interrupted me, "Dad, I'm done with this!" He exclaimed.

"I'm tired of being the one to look after you! Ever since, Caidwall; you've been drinking and you quit your job!" He yelled, disappointment and frustration pouring from his words. Before Jason could continue his rant, I knocked out completely. I wish I never took up drinking and never made Jason go through this.

The next morning, I woke up with a killer headache, "Ah, fuck me." I said holding my head due to the pain. I got up and went to my kitchen to take my pills; After I almost met Sir Death himself last time In Evelyn's car then at Fairweather's estate, I decided to get pills to treat my blood pressure.

I then remembered what happened the night before, and how Jason was angry at me. I immediately felt a surge of guilt so I proceeded upstairs to apologize to Jason. I walked into his bedroom only to see he wasn't there, "Jason!" I yelled hoping to get a response. However, the silence denied me it.

I looked throughout the room hoping to find a clue on where Jason was. I felt anxious and worried, what if Caidwall had him again? My fears came to an ease as I saw a note in Jason's handwriting. It said "I'm frustrated, Dad. I want us to have a better relationship, but it feels impossible with the way things are. I need a break, when you're done with this drinking nonsense, find me at Grandma's house."

I closed up the note, and fell down to my knees in tears; I was affecting my son so much because of my own guilt and regret. I thought about who I've been lately. The city has been in deep shit since I let Caidwall win that day; protests, increased crime rate, low income homes not surviving, my son drifting away from me, my alcoholism and it's all because of me. Because I let Caidwall win.

I proceeded down the stairs and rushed to my phone; I dialed my mom's number. I haven't talked to her in a while; my mom was an amazing Muslim mom but after I got married, I steered away from her to focus on the Everhaven Chronicles and my family and ended up losing contact with her. What a waste that turned out to be. Though I was born in a Muslim family, I never really was too religious. Aliah was Christian and after I married her I stopped practicing Islam. I called my mom, and she said, "Hello?" She said into the phone, I hadn't heard my mom's sweet and gentle voice in awhile so it was a nice change of pace from what I had been through.

"Mom, it's Alex," I said. "Mom is Jason ok-" she interrupted "Assalaamulaikum, Alex. I haven't heard from you in a while, how are you?" She said, her words dripping with love. I spoke up, "I'm okay, where's Jaso-" she interrupted again, "I have Jason here, he told me what happened."

Instantly, guilt washed over me like a tidal wave, weighing heavily on my shoulders. "I'm sorry about Jason," I murmured, my voice heavy with regret, as I tried to mask my sadness.

Evelyn's response was gentle, her words a balm to my troubled soul. "Darling, the Almighty knows your struggles, and I empathize with what you're going through. Please, think about Jason's well-being and let's work together to bring this to an end. Your family deserves a brighter future," she said, her voice filled with compassion.

"Aliah would have never wanted this," she added, her words resonating with me as she tried to reason with me. It was a sobering reminder of the stakes involved and the importance of considering Jason's welfare above all else.

I stood there, the weight of my guilt pressing down on me like a ton of bricks. Thoughts of Jason, the people I've betrayed, and Aliah swirled in my mind, each one a painful reminder of my actions. A lump formed in my throat as tears welled up in my eyes, my emotions finally breaking free after being bottled up for so long.

My mother's voice cut through the silence, her words carrying a mixture of concern and understanding. "Look, I know you're struggling, Alex," she said, her tone gentle yet firm. "But you need to find a way to deal with this guilt. Go to the mosque, pour your heart out to Allah. It might help you find some peace."

Her suggestion struck a chord with me, offering a glimmer of hope in the darkness.

"Yeah, maybe you're right," I replied, my voice choked with emotion. "I'll give it a shot. Thanks, Mom."

I put the phone away and sat down for a minute; I thought about all that has happened in the last year. Could this be good for me? Is God the answer to my problems? I didn't know what to do; I felt like I was too far gone and that the big man above wouldn't forgive me. I then sat down on the couch, "I need to do better. For Jason, for Aliah." I thought to myself.

I then got up, and proceeded to the front of my house to get in my car. Imagine my surprise when I see no car in my driveway, "Really? Jason took the car?" I muttered under my breath. I then searched up on google maps how far the nearest mosque was from my home. "10 minutes by walk?" I accidentally exclaimed out loud, "Eh, I need the exercise anyways."

As I made my way through Haven Square, dodging the protesters and trying to avoid Caidwall's smug gaze, I couldn't help but feel like a character in some twisted sitcom. Caidwall then saw me amongst the crowd "Ah yes, Alex Hawthorne, the journalist with a heart of stone," Caidwall said with sarcasm, referring to Evelyn.

But beneath the humor, a deep sense of frustration simmered. Caidwall's empty promises, political theatrics, and sarcasm were enough to make anyone's blood boil. And as much as I wanted to give him a piece of my mind, I knew better than to take the bait. "Not today, Caidwall," I muttered, keeping my cool as I pushed through the crowd.

Another 5 minutes passed and I finally reached the mosque. I couldn't help but feel a sense of relief wash over me. Stepping inside, I let out a sigh of relief, grateful for the brief respite from the chaos of the outside world. "Well, this is a nice change of pace," I joked to myself, sinking into a nearby pew.

I entered the mosque and saw a bunch of guys coming in, they took off their shoes and put it on what seemed to be a shoe rack so I did the same. I remembered from my childhood that before prayer, we had to cleanse ourselves with water. So I proceeded to the washroom to perform ablution; As I tried to remember how to do ablution, the man performing it beside me seemed to notice I was struggling, "You new here?" he said as he peered at me. I tried to look as casual as possible, but I didn't know what to say, "Uh... N- No, not exactly, but I forg-" he interrupted me "Hey, it's okay, we don't judge." he said with care. "I got you."

Surprised by his generosity, I said, "Thank you so much."

He then started showing me how to perform ablution. "Okay, so first you gotta say, 'bismillah'" I repeated after him but fumbled on the words, "Bis- mahlah?"

He started laughing, "Haha, don't worry you'll get it." He said as he began his demonstration, "To start, rinse your mouth three times, then use water to wipe your nose and face three times each. After that, give each arm a good rinse up to the elbow, moving on to your face, hair, and the insides of your ears with the water. Finish up by washing your right foot and then repeating the process with your left foot."

I repeated the process, "Any other questions, ask me. I'll be more than happy to help you." The man said. I was very surprised by him and his generosity; I came in there expecting glaring eyes of shame and disappointment. However, this man showed me that they didn't do that there.

I followed him, and he led the prayer; as I struggled to learn how to pray again, I bowed my head down and the weight of my guilt and uncertainty crept back in. I may have cracked a few jokes along the way, but deep down, I knew that I had a lot of soul-searching to do.

The prayer ended and everyone threw their hands up in prayer. I started talking to god, "Allah, I- I'm sorry, I made the wrong decision; I should have tried to help Evelyn and the rest. I wish I never took up drinking and made a bad impact on Jason. I don't know if you're going to forgive someone like me." I said as tears started dropping from my eyes, "But please don't make it hard on Jason."

The guy who taught me how to do ablution sat down in front of me. I wiped my eyes and he asked, "Hey, I never caught your name." I grinned, "I'm Alex." He offered a handshake, "Assalaamulaikum Alex, I'm Ali," he said, smiling. His friendly demeanor eased my personal struggles. Sitting comfortably, he asked, "New to Islam, brother Alex?" I replied, "Sort of. I grew up Muslim, but after getting married, I kinda drifted away to focus on my career." He looked curious, "So, what brought you back to our lord?" I hesitated, should I have told him that I betrayed people that trusted me? That I betrayed my son? That I did god awful things?

Ali saw my silence and understood immediately, "Ah, I see." He said looking towards the front of the mosque.

I gave him a puzzled look, "Huh? I didn't say anything." He laid his hand on my shoulder, "You didn't need to. We've all messed up; we've all sinned." Guilt sank in, "I've gone too far, Ali. I'm beyond forgiveness."

Ali dropped a wisdom bomb, "Alex, every chapter in our holy book, the Quran, starts with something. Do you know what?" I had no clue, "No, what does it start with?" He got ready, "Bismillahir Rahmanir Raheem," he said. I looked at him, confused but trying not to be rude. "It means 'In the name of God, Most Gracious, Most Merciful.' The Quran teaches us that God is super merciful and forgives all."

I sat there quietly, absorbing Ali's words. "Chapter 11, verse 52 of the Quran talks about asking for forgiveness, and you'll be showered with forgiveness, happiness, and strength," he said, continuing, "Alex, God will always forgive you. Don't ever think you're beyond that." Ali got up, saying, "You're not defined by the tragedies of the past; but of trust in the future. God has a plan for you filled with the happiness that you desire." He glanced back at me, finding me teary-eyed. I wiped my tears, "Thanks, man. You're one hell of a guy."

"Don't give up. I'll share my number later. Let's stay in touch," he said, walking away.

I looked ahead in the mosque, and for the first time in a while, I smiled.

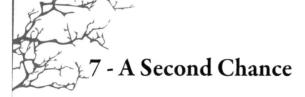

7 - A Second Chance

Slumping into my couch after the mosque, thoughts of God swirling in my head, I muttered a quiet "Thanks, Allah."

Then it hit me: Mom wanted a post-mosque debrief. As I dragged myself toward my phone, it suddenly lit up like a Christmas tree. Who in their right mind would be calling now? Heart racing, I answered cautiously, "Hello?"

And wouldn't you know it, it was the same spine-chilling voice—the guy who dumped that cursed Eris Stoneheart shit in my lap, flipping my life upside down. "Hello, Alex," he said.

"Listen, man, I just went on a whole ass self-discovery journey. Whatever shady business you're into, just put a damn pin in it," I retorted, trying to keep a lid on the panic brewing inside.

But nope, Mr. Nightmare Fuel wasn't having any of it. He just dropped a bombshell: "15 East End Street, one hour." And with that, he hung up, leaving me cussing up a storm and dreading the memories that address stirred up—it was the old base of operations for Evelyn, Crissy, and Jacob. I felt my guilt and anxiety slowly peek through as I was reminded by memories of the three and how bad I did by them.

I hesitated leaving my house, I didn't want another case from the mystery man. I was tired and I just wanted to spend my time away from the stress and the guilt; spending time trying to better myself for my family. "Ah, fuck it." I muttered as I made the brave yet stupid decision to go back to "The Everhaven Times."

I searched up how far it is by walking and it was 45 flipping minutes long. "Eh, I got enough exercise today." I jokingly muttered as I proceeded to call an Uber. On the drive there, I couldn't help but wonder, Who was this mystery man? What were his ties to the corruption in Everhaven? And, why did he choose *me* to help stop it?

After a tense hour, I arrived at the apartment. I thanked the uber driver and got out of the car, he then drove off. I looked up at the apartment in sadness, the once hideout to fight corruption in this city, was turned into a complete waste area. Pieces of garbage and trash all over the street near the building; and it was all because of me. I then proceeded to walk inside to face the music, I walked up the stairs to the base. After an anxious 20 minutes, I arrived at the door of the Everhaven Times. I braced myself as I opened the door for the guilt I was about to feel; I opened the door and saw the horror. I saw monitors and table items on the floor, it was my fault that they were taken and my fault that the state of the apartment was like this.

I looked through the mess and saw a picture of the three. My eyes swelled up, but as my eyes began shedding tears, I heard a loud noise coming from the corner. I quickly wiped my eyes and turned around facing the corner, "Jesus, don't scare me like that." I yelled out. A man stepped out from the corner, in a long trench coat and a tall hat, "I thought *I* was Sherlock Holmes." I jokingly muttered under my breath. "Hello Alex, it's about time we met." The man said, I started feeling anxious. Was the mysterious man an ally? Or a foe?

The man saw my anxiety and reassured me, "Ah, don't worry. I'm here to help; my name is Donovan Caidwall."

I lashed out at his surname, "Get the fuck away from me." I exclaimed as I backed up. The man tried calming me down, but I didn't want my life to be messed up even further. "Alex, relax. I'm the one who sent you the call last year." He said referring to the case of Eris Stoneheart. I tried telling him off, "I don't want anything to do with you! The mayor has already fucked my life up!" I exclaimed.

"I'm sorry about my father." Donovan said.

I then felt a surge of rage and pure anger, "He... Mayor Caldwall is your father?" I said, my hands beginning to close up. I didn't trust Donovan, I didn't want any more problems in my life coming from the mayor. He peered at me trying to get me to relax, "I'm nothing like my father. I haven't talked to him in 6 years, I'm here to protect Everhaven from him." He said, throwing his hands up, trying to ease my mind.

I slightly calmed down, "What do you need from me? I'm not partaking in any other bullshit case you have for me. Not after what happened last year." I said as I began to walk out the door. He then held my arm trying to plead with me, "Alex, you have to! My father is planning to turn this city into a fuckin' cash cow. He's demolishing homes and apartments to turn them into casinos and offices! We have to expose him, and the dirty asshole he is."

I thought about it for a minute, I couldn't bear to put Jason through another mess involving Mayor Douche again. I pulled his hand off of my arm and stormed off. "Get your hand off my *fuckin'* arm." I said. As I proceeded to exit out the door, Donovan said something to me that I thought I would never hear, "We can get the Everhaven times team back." He yelled out to me. I froze for a minute, I thought about my betrayal and if there was really a way— a *chance* to set things right. I looked back at Donovan, "What are you talking about?" I said.

"I know where Caidwall is holding the gang. We gotta bust them out if we wanna take him down," Donovan said, flipping through a file like a pro detective.

He thrust the evidence at me. "Check it out, all the dirt on the mayor. We can nail him once and for all, dude."

Trying to win me over, he laid it on thick. "Alex, I'm nothing like my old man. He tried to groom me into his mini-me, but after what he did to Mayor Fairweather, I had to draw the line."

I sighed, looking down for a moment before meeting his gaze again. "Listen, the Mayor took my kid hostage last year. I can't risk that again. Sure, let's get back what we lost, but I gotta protect what I've got left. At all costs."

I took a step closer, trying to lighten the mood. "And maybe let's shoot for not ending up in a body bag, huh?" I quipped, trying to inject a bit of humor into the heavy situation.

Donovan smirked, "Deal, let's get to work."

Donovan's smirk widened into a determined grin. "Alright, here's the plan," he began, his voice steady as he laid out each step with precision.

"Crissy, Jacob, and Evelyn are being held in an underground prison on the outskirts of Everhaven City. It's heavily guarded, but I've managed to gather some intel on the security protocols."

He pulled out a map, pointing to various entry points and patrol routes. "We'll need to approach from the east side, where the security is slightly less fortified. Once we're inside, you'll be dressing up as a security guard to blend in and make your way to the holding area."

My eyebrows shot up in surprise. Dressing up as a security guard? That was some next-level undercover work. But Donovan seemed confident in the plan. Donovan's grin faltered for a moment as he noticed my surprise. "I know it's a risky move, Alex," he admitted, his voice tinged with understanding. "But it's the only way to get Crissy, Jacob, and Evelyn out of there."

I swallowed hard, the reality of breaking into a heavily guarded prison sinking in. The thought of sneaking past armed guards and navigating unknown territory made my stomach churn with apprehension.

But before I could voice my concerns, Donovan reassured me. "Don't worry, Alex. I'll have your back every step of the way," he said, his tone firm with conviction. "You won't be going in unarmed. I'll make sure you're equipped with a stun gun for protection, and I'll be in your ear via comms the entire time."

His words brought a glimmer of reassurance amidst the uncertainty. With Donovan guiding me and providing support, maybe breaking into the prison wasn't as daunting as it seemed.

"As for me," Donovan continued, "I'll be your eyes and ears on the outside, guiding you through the facility and providing backup if things go south. We'll need to move quickly and quietly to avoid detection."

I nodded, absorbing the details of the plan. It was risky, but if it meant rescuing Crissy, Jacob, and Evelyn and bringing down Mayor Caldwall, it was a risk worth taking.

"Alright, let's do this," I said, determination burning in my chest. "We'll get the team back and take down that corrupt sonuvabitch once and for all."

Donovan grinned, a glimmer of excitement in his eyes, muttered under his mouth, "I'm coming for you, dad."

With a newfound sense of purpose, we set off to execute Donovan's plan, ready to face whatever challenges came our way. It was time to bring justice to Everhaven. And fix my mistakes along the way.

8 - Doing The Impossible

With comms crackling in my ear, I whined to Donovan, "Seriously, this security guard outfit is tighter than my mom's grip on her purse. I'm never complaining about my regular clothing again.."

"Don't let fashion be the reason you get caught, Alex. Focus on the mission," Donovan quipped back, injecting a hint of humor into the seriousness.

Unlocking the door with a swipe of the security card, I strolled past guards eyeing me like I was the newest circus act. "Tight uniform, tight situation," I muttered, unable to resist cracking a joke.

"Don't give them a stand-up routine, Alex. Find that camera feed room," Donovan's voice teased. Spotting a superior guard, I played the rookie card, "I'm new, and the boss is already on my case. Where's the camera feed room?"

The superior guard sighed, pointing down the hall, "You should know this, rookie. It's over there."

"Thank you, sir." I mumbled. I walked down the hall and entered the camera feed room. I Instantly spotted an officer engrossed in the monitors, I tapped his shoulder, delivering a knockout performance before stashing him in a closet.

"Good shit, Alex. Now, let's turn this into a rescue operation," Donovan quipped in my ear. As I manipulated the cameras, I couldn't help but mutter, "If this works, I'll forgive you for the fashion advice, Donovan."

"Don't thank me yet; we've still got a rescue to pull off," Donovan chuckled, keeping the atmosphere light in the midst of tension.

As I played spy with the camera feeds, there they were – Crissy, Jacob, and Evelyn, all stuck in Prisoner Block 07.

"Found 'em," I whispered into the comms, trying to sound cool while my nerves were doing the cha-cha. Donovan's voice came through, "Nice one, Alex. Now, let's cook up a plan to spring them free."

I scrutinized the room like I was Sherlock solving a case, but honestly, I was just a guy in a tight uniform trying not to mess this up more than I already have. Donovan's guidance cut in, "Don't lose it now. I'm downloading a blueprint on that block. Working on a plan based on the blueprint right now. Just hold tight."

Staring at the monitors, I imagined their faces looking back at me – disappointment, anger, maybe a touch of "Seriously, Alex?" I muttered to myself, "You're in deep shit, buddy. Just hope they've got a sprinkle of forgiveness left."

In the midst of the spy game, guilt crept in like an uninvited guest. I had some serious explaining to do, and I wasn't sure if my friends would be up for a forgiving chat.

Urgency turned into a drummer pounding in my chest. Getting my friends out was the goal, but facing them after my betrayal? That was the elephant in the room. I gulped, "Okay, plan, step 1: pretend I know what I'm doing, step 2: look confident, and lastly hope that nobody notices the guy in the tight security guard costume."

"No- wha- Alex" Donovan exclaimed in my ear, I ignored him as I set off for Prisoner Block 07. I walked through the hall, my nerves pumping with each step. It felt like I was Batman but without the fancy gadgets and tragic backstory.

I arrived at the entrance of Prisoner Block 07. I readied myself for whatever was behind the door, whether it be the disappointed looks on the people I thought were dead faces or any security guards with assault rifles. "Bismillah." I muttered under my breath as the door opened by itself, I walked through, and I saw 4 security guards with assault rifles; my heart started racing again, like what happened at Fairweather's house. I struggled to breathe a little, "Alex! You good?" Donovan chimed in my ear, I calmed myself down and continued to walk, I muttered, "Yep!"

I walked past the guards and arrived at the cell. I stood in front of the cave, and saw all three of them, I— I froze. Suddenly, the world around me just froze. The people I betrayed were right in front me and they've been in this prison for a year. It was my fault, all my fault.

"Snap the fuck out of it!" Donovan yelled in my ear, I quickly regained focus and knocked on the cell.

The trio was lounging like they were on a tropical vacation until they spotted me. I casually approached the cell, doing my best secret agent swagger while unlocking the door.

"Hey! Rookie! What are you doing?!" A guard barked, and I panicked for a hot second, but then I channeled my inner action hero. "We got word there might be an attempt to break them out. Mayor wants them relocated," I blurted, hoping I sounded more confident than I felt.

"Let's get bossman in here," another guard suggested. Frantically brainstorming an excuse, I blurted out, "Unless y'all wanna be the reason the mayor goes down, and trust me, you don't want that. I suggest you let me relocate them."

The guards exchanged puzzled glances and then collectively shrugged, saying, "Fine." I unlocked the cell, putting on my best drill sergeant act, "All of you, get up! Now!"

Evelyn rose first, followed by Jacob and Crissy. They hadn't recognized me yet, and I started herding them down the hall. Muttering to myself, I said, "Donovan, I can't believe that worked." Donovan's cheer in my ear felt like a touchdown at the Super Bowl. "Yes! Okay, just go out the way you came in."

Then Crissy, all grown-up at 17, looked at me and started, "Hey, isn't that Ale-" Evelyn and Jacob jumped in faster than a cat on a laser pointer, covering her mouth. They recognized me, and the disappointment on their faces hit me like stepping on a Lego.

"We're almost out," I said with a heavy sigh. Evelyn shot me a glare, "Fuck you." She exclaimed. Her words cut deeper than a knife. We passed the camera feed room, and suddenly, Mr. Knocked-Out-Guard walked out.

He pointed at me like he'd found Waldo, "INTRUDER!" He yelled.

Evelyn screamed, "What the hell are we waiting for?! Run!" We sprinted towards the exit, but guards swarmed in. "Donovan! Where do we go?" I yelled into the comms. Donovan, in full panic mode, checked the blueprints, "Shit! Shit! Okay, go left!"

So, left we went, me signaling the group like a traffic cop. Guards started shooting like it was Assault Rifle Appreciation Day. Crissy quipped, "What is this?! Fuckin' Assault Rifle appreciation day?"

"Left again!" Donovan screamed into the comms. "Now, make a right!"

We finally reached another exit, but it was like the universe was playing a prank – broken and shut. "Jacob! Help me get this open!" I hollered. He joined in, and we yanked the door like we were in a tug-of-war.

"They're fucking gaining on us!" Evelyn yelled, capturing the essence of our grand escape. In the deafening chaos, Jacob froze for a moment, his eyes reflecting the apprehension that gripped him. I saw the hesitation etched across his face, then his gaze fell upon my stun gun. Without a second thought, he snatched it up. "What are you doing?!" I yelled, desperation in my voice. He pointed the gun toward the oncoming guards. "Buying you guys time."

Evelyn rushed to help me while Crissy shouted at Jacob, her voice heavy with fear, "Jacob, no! You're going to die!" The guards closed in, and Jacob, an unexpected hero, started firing, taking them down one by one. Meanwhile, Evelyn pulled Crissy outside, her grip firm as she tried to shield her from the unfolding tragedy.

One of the rifle's bullets found its mark on Jacob's leg, then his arm, and finally, his stomach. He crumpled to the ground, and Crissy's cry pierced the chaotic air. "NO!" she screamed, her anguish echoing in the night.

I couldn't leave him to die, not like this. Without hesitation, I rushed to Jacob's side, hoisted him up, and carried him outside.

Bullets from the guards' assault rifles rained down on us as I got him by my vehicle. I pressed the button, sealing us in, and gently laid him on the ground. Evelyn and Crissy surrounded him, their eyes filled with terror and grief.

Crissy, unable to contain her sorrow, broke into tears. Evelyn, with her own tears streaming down, pulled Crissy away, shielding her from the heartbreaking sight. I knelt by Jacob's side, the weight of guilt and regret heavy in my chest. "I—Jacob, I don't—" he interrupted me, his weakening voice struggling to convey his thoughts. "I never thought it would end like this, Alex. A year we spent behind those walls, and you... you were the last person I expected to betray us. Was it worth it? Was it worth everything we lost?"

His grip tightened on my shirt, and he peered at Evelyn and Crissy, their tears mirroring his pain. "I forgive you. But please take care of them. Don't fuck it up again, and promise me that you'll take down that evil sonuvabitch, Caidwall." Jacob said as I promised him to do so he then called over Crissy and Evelyn, "I was someone working for a corrupt corporation, and I lost myself for a while. But you two, showed me who I truly was. You made my life beautiful, I love you guys, always." With those poignant words, Jacob drew his final breath. Tears welled up in my eyes as I felt the profound weight of his forgiveness and his plea for the safety of our friends.

The door began to open again, guards regaining control. I swiftly ushered Evelyn and Crissy into the car, and we drove off into the night, bullets ricocheting off the vehicle. Crissy, inconsolable, wept uncontrollably, and Evelyn, with teary eyes, tried to comfort her.

Jacob had sacrificed his life for us, for Everhaven. I knew his blood stained my hands, and I vowed to ensure his death wouldn't be in vain.

As we sped away from the scene, Jacob's sacrifice fueled my determination to stop Mayor Caidwall's rise to power, whatever it took. In the quiet of the night, with grief heavy in our hearts, we drove forward into an uncertain future.

9 - Death In The Family

Evelyn and Crissy sat back at the Everhaven Times base, their eyes filled with agony, sadness, and tears over losing someone like family. I stood there, weary, knowing all this pain stemmed from Caidwall's lust for power. Donovan broke the heavy silence, "We're going to take him down. I have a plan, guys."

Attempting reassurance, I said, "We're going to make sure Jacob's death isn't in va-" but Crissy interrupted, screaming, "Shut the *fuck* up! What makes you think we'll trust you again after what you did to us?! You go Jacob fuckin' killed!"

Evelyn walked up, and as I sought forgiveness in her eyes, she slapped me. "Yep, deserved that," I muttered. "We thought— *I thought* I could trust you," she exclaimed. "You're just like all these corrupt journalists."

Crissy peered at me and then at Donovan, questioning, "What's with Sherlock Holmes?" Donovan, bracing himself, revealed, "My name is Donovan Caidwall." Their eyes widened in surprise at his surname. "I want to take down my father; Everhaven deserves better than his brand of leadership."

As Donovan explained his plan, Evelyn walked toward him, stating, "I trust you more than this turncoat right now." I put my head down in sadness, uncertain how to earn their forgiveness. In the following week, I kept trying, but they weren't letting up.

Donovan explained that in the next week that Caidwall was revealing a new office building and then there, we would make a move to show everyone what kind of mayor Richard Caidwall truly was. "We're going to get in, put this on the control panel." Donovan said as he held up a USB stick drive, "This drive is connected to my microphone, so the day of the public reveal, we say a couple of words, and boom! Mission accomplished." Donovan excitedly said.

Evelyn got confused, "Who's sneaking in?" she said. Donovan looked at me with joy in his eyes. I hesitated, "Hey, I'm not dressing up again!"

Throughout that entire week, Donovan shared more details on his plan to expose the mayor during the public reveal of the new office building. I persisted in seeking forgiveness from Evelyn and Crissy, but deep inside, I knew I had a lot of asking for forgiveness to do. On the day to sneak into the new offices, I asked Donovan, "Remind me again, why do *I* have to do this?" Nerves pumping, he reassured me, "Don't worry, this time, you don't gotta wear a tight outfit."

Frustrated, I looked at him, "But I gotta sneak through a heavily guarded building," as he equipped cameras to my body suit, handing me a stun gun and a baton. "You got a pep talk for sneaking into a guarded building?" I joked.

Donovan, taken aback, couldn't find words. "It's alright," I chuckled, putting my hand on his shoulder. And I set off, I looked back at Crissy and Evelyn once more to try to get a reaction, anything. But they put their heads down in anger...

An hour later, I reached the other side of Everhaven, where the building was going to be revealed to the public the next day. "Let's take down Backhead Benny, yeah?" I said to communications. Crissy, still disappointed in me, said, "Whatever." However Evelyn stayed quiet.

"Okay, you're going to head in from the side entrance. It's the only entrance in the entire building that's not heavily guarded. However, when you are inside, it's going to get very complicated." Donovan said in communications. I hesitated, but Donovan, like always, reassured me, "It's like last time, but I'm here if anything goes south." He said.

I spoke into the communications with a glimmer of hope, "Evelyn, Crissy. I know there's nothing I can say that will make you forgive me; but I want you guys to know that whatever happens, it's been an honor working with you guys. Especially you Evelyn, you brought out a part of me that I've kept buried ever since my wife died. I'll always be grateful for that." I said as I started to walk towards the side entrance, "I know you two aren't talking to me but I also wanted to letchu' know that I promise that I'm not going let Jacob's death be in vain, I made him a promise to protect you guys and take down the mayor; and I'm going to live to see it through."

I then proceeded to enter through the side entrance, my heart filled with hope that this would work out and that Caidwall's regime would fall. I entered and proceeded to go up the stairs to see 2 guards pass me, I ducked so that they wouldn't see me.

Stealth mode engaged, I tip-toed through the guarded building, feeling like a spy in a cheesy action movie. The distant murmur of conversations added a soundtrack to my clandestine mission, making me half-expect the *Mission Impossible* theme to start playing.

Locating the entrance to the control room, I slipped through the shadows like a ninja avoiding laser beams—okay, maybe not lasers, but you get the vibe. The room was alive with the soft glow of screens and the electronic hum of gadgets. It was like being in a tech-savvy superhero's lair, minus the capes.

Approaching the control panel, I glanced over my shoulder to make sure I wasn't starring in my own version of "Caught on Camera." Mission accomplished, I strategically placed the USB drive at the back of the speaker, feeling a weird mix of secret agent and amateur radio host vibes.

As I proceeded to exit the control room, I half-expected a voice in my earpiece saying, "Good job, Agent Alex." Navigating back through the maze of the building, my determination was fueled by the thought of the day after's showdown with the corrupt mayor.

The microphone, my not-so-secret weapon, held the potential to expose the mayor's shadiness. It wasn't just about taking down a bad guy; it was like being part of a wild plot twist in the city's story.

Each step echoed a commitment to rebuild trust, restore faith, and, let's not forget, fulfill the promise to honor Jacob's memory. The night continued, a quirky prelude to the big reveal, and I couldn't help but think, "Well, this is one way to shake up a city."

As I exited the control room, I heard 2 guards conversing and coming my way. As I slinked back into the control room like a ninja in a cheesy action flick, I strained my ears to catch the guards' conversation. Seriously, it was like listening to a podcast you didn't subscribe to but couldn't turn off.

One guard, probably the philosophical type, dropped a bombshell question, asking his buddy if he ever felt guilty working for a corrupt politician. The other guard's response? Classic. He basically said, "Nah, bro, I traded my soul for a six-figure paycheck. Worth it, right?" The guards burst out laughing.

And there I was, contemplating the seductive allure of six figures, like it was a shiny lure dangling in front of a fish. "I could really use the—" Nah, I stopped myself. Principles, man. Can't buy those on Amazon Prime.

Just when I thought I had a moment to catch my breath, Donovan's voice crackled over the comm. "Hey, Alex, guess what? Mayor's in the building, with his posse. And sorry to rain on your parade, but taking the stairwell back down? Not recommended."

Great. Just what I needed. A VIP visit and a stairwell embargo. My life's like a sitcom, but without the laugh track. Time to brainstorm my next move, preferably one that doesn't involve running into the corrupt politician's entourage or getting cozy with a paycheck that's as dirty as their deeds.

As I took in Donovan's warning, I couldn't help but feel like the universe was conspiring against me. Mayor and his entourage on one side, guards blocking my exit on the other. It was like being stuck between a rock and a hard place, with a side order of corrupt politics.

But hey, if there's one thing I've learned from binge-watching crime dramas, it's that there's always a way out.

I just had to find it. So, with a deep breath and a mental pep talk, I started plotting my escape.

First things first, I needed to gather intel. I scanned the room for any tools or gadgets that could give me an edge. Sure, I wasn't exactly James Bond, but a little creativity can go a long way.

Then, I remembered the ventilation shaft. It was a long shot, but desperate times called for desperate measures. "Donovan, you got plans on the ventilation system in the building?" I asked Donovan on communications. He said he did and agreed to guide me through it. With a silent "bismillah" that it wouldn't collapse under my weight, I pried open the vent cover and hoisted myself inside.

As Donovan was giving me directions and crawling through the cramped space, I felt like a human-sized mouse in a maze. But I pushed aside the claustrophobia and focused on the task at hand. Inch by inch, I made my way towards freedom, dodging dust bunnies and the occasional spider.

Finally, after what felt like an eternity, I emerged on the other side, blinking in the harsh fluorescent light of the hallway. I was free. Well, sort of. I still had to navigate past the guards and the mayor's entourage, but hey, at least I had a fighting chance.

As I briskly walked through the corridor, another set of guards appeared, blocking my path like oversized chess pieces. My heart skipped a beat as I realized my escape route was cut off.

Thinking quickly, I ducked into the nearest office, praying it wasn't occupied. The room was dimly lit, with a cluttered desk and a few chairs scattered around. I pressed myself against the wall, trying to make myself as inconspicuous as possible.

But luck wasn't on my side. Just as I began to relax, I heard the faint sound of footsteps approaching. Panic surged through me as I realized the guards were heading straight for the office.

"Uh, guys, little help here?" I whispered frantically into my comm, hoping Donovan or someone would come up with a genius plan to get me out of this mess. Evelyn, Crissy, and Donovan all chimed in, their voices a jumble of concern and frantic brainstorming. But before they could come up with a plan, I made a split-second decision.

"I'm jumping out a window," I blurted out, my voice surprisingly calm considering the insanity of the situation. There was a brief moment of stunned silence before Evelyn protested, "Alex, wait, that's crazy!" But I didn't have time to argue. With a determined breath, I swung the window open and leaped out, grabbing onto the railing just in time, set over the traffic below. For a terrifying moment, I dangled precariously below the window, praying that my grip would hold. Above me, the guards entered the room, their footsteps echoing ominously. "Don't look down, don't look down," I muttered under my breath, trying to keep my nerves in check. But of course, one of the guards couldn't resist. He peered out the window, his gaze locking onto mine with a mixture of shock and disbelief.

For a heartbeat, time seemed to stand still. Then, with a casual shrug, the guard closed the window, dismissing me as nothing more than a trick of the light. As the footsteps faded away, I let out a shaky breath, relief flooding through me. But then I looked down, "Shit!" I exclaimed as I climbed up pressing my body against the wall. "How am I getting out of this one?" I frantically muttered to myself looking over the traffic of Everhaven. "Are you okay?!" Evelyn asked me, I slightly smiled at her concern, "Yeah" I said as I climbed down to the next window. I then climbed into the window, and fell to the ground; my heart pumping fast. I let myself cool down, and got back up.

As I made my way out of the office and proceeded down the stairwell, I realized I was on the bottom floor. The front desk was in front of me on the right and the front door, in all it's glory, was on the left. I let go of the tension in my back and proceeded to the front door. However, I heard people conversing coming my way. So, I frantically hid under the front desk. Then, I heard him... Caidwall, he was talking to his personal security guard, "Get the control room ready for the public reveal. We're making American history starting tomorrow." Caidwall said as he put something on the table above. I curled myself into a ball, hoping that he wouldn't see me. He went back to his guard and the guard started speaking, "Sir, what would you like us to do about Jacob Clariegiven's body?"

"Get rid of it, it's of no use to me." Caidwall replied as they both walked upstairs, past me. I felt my blood boil and my fists close. How could he do this to Jacob? To just dispose of his body? I completely forgot that the whole team could hear what was going on, "When I get my hands on that dickwad-" Crissy exclaimed. Donovan reassured her, "All in due time." He said.

I calmed myself down and got back up, I saw what Caidwall placed on top of the front desk; they were documents, I picked them up and started shuffling through them. "Looks like Caidwall is planning to move up to the White House. Guys, with his connections to the White House, he wants to buy out the guys over there." I said shuffling, "Donovan, why is your dad so interested in the White House? And how does he have so many connections to the guys over there?"

Donovan let out a big sigh, "As I grew up, he told me plans of taking over the country. He wants power because he feels like America needs order, his type of order. So with people he met that are situated there, he set out on his plan. But when Fairweather died, I knew I couldn't sit on the sidelines anymore." He said sadfully. I could tell what type of person the mayor truly was through Donovan's feelings.

I put the documents down, "We stop all of this tomorrow." I said as I sprinted out the front door. I got in my car and drove off; As I started driving back to the Everhaven Times, I couldn't help but think about how I almost fuckin' died jumping out of a window. And of course, if our efforts would be enough to stop Richard Caidwall and his rise to power. I couldn't let Jacob's death be for no reason, and I made him a promise; one that I intended to keep.

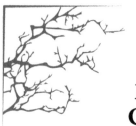

10 - Jacob Claregiven

As I entered the Everhaven Times office, Donovan practically danced with glee. "Yes!" he cheered, his excitement contagious enough to make even the most cynical among us crack a smile. Then came Crissy, charging at me like a linebacker on game day. I braced myself for impact, fully expecting her trademark fiery wrath. But instead of a verbal beatdown, she surprised me with a bone-crushing hug. "Don't you dare pull a stunt like that again!" she scolded, punctuating her words with a playful punch to my arm.

"Hey, no promises," I quipped, earning myself another playful smack before she pulled me in for another hug. I told myself: maybe lay off the death-defying stunts for a while.

I looked to Evelyn hoping for the same forgiveness but she remained unmoved by the emotional rollercoaster unfolding before her. My heart dropped a little, I didn't know if she would ever forgive me.

Meanwhile, Donovan was rallying the troops like a coach giving a pre-game pep talk. "We're gonna take down that sonuvabitch once and for all!" he declared, his eyes shining with determination.

We exchanged determined glances, ready to take on whatever challenges lay ahead. "Alright, what's the game plan, coach?" I asked, eager to get started. With Donovan leading the charge and Crissy's fiery spirit at our side, there was no way we could lose. Well, hopefully.

Donovan, ever the mastermind, laid out our strategy with the precision of a seasoned tactician. "We've got the evidence, now it's time to unleash it like a pack of hungry wolves. We'll hit 'em with everything we've got: front-page exposés, hard-hitting investigative pieces, you name it. We're gonna make sure the whole city knows what this guy's been up to."

Crissy cracked her knuckles, her eyes gleaming with anticipation. "Consider it done. No stone unturned, no detail overlooked. We're gonna blow the lid off this thing."

Evelyn nodded in agreement, her expression determined. "Let's show 'em what real journalism looks like."

And with that, we got to work, our fingers flying across keyboards and phones ringing off the hook as we pieced together the story that would shake Everhaven to its core. It was gonna be one hell of a ride; but if there was one thing I knew for sure, it was that Caidwall was going to go down, one way or the other.

As the day dragged on, our efforts to gather support and strategize continued. Phones rang incessantly, papers shuffled, and fingers tapped away at keyboards, as we meticulously planned our next move.

With each call, we leaned on every favor owed to us, and with each discussion, we pieced together a plan that would shake the foundation of Caidwall's corruption. But amid the chaos, there were moments of levity.

"Donovan, We could go into the spy business. We've got the stealth and the drama down pat," I quipped, earning a chuckle from him.

Crissy, always ready with a sharp retort, chimed in, "Yeah, except we're way too honest for that. Plus, I don't think our budget could handle all the fancy gadgets." Evelyn didn't let out any laughter, I could tell she was still angry at me.

Donovan, ever the captain of our ship, grinned. "Alright, enough joking around, people. Let's stay focused. We've got a corrupt politician to take down, and we're not stopping until my dad gets what's coming for him.

As the night crept on and our weary bodies finally surrendered to sleep, my mind couldn't shake the haunting images of my nightmare. In the darkness, I found myself back in the clutches of fear, reliving the moment when Caidwall snatched away everything I held dear.

I woke up startled, the echoes of his chilling words still ringing in my ears. "You are not enough," he taunted, his voice a venomous whisper in the silence of my room. I woke up to see Evelyn by my side seemingly comforting me while I had my nightmare.

"Evelyn?" I called out, my voice hoarse with panic. "What are you doing up?"

Her eyes met mine, reflecting the same turmoil that churned within me. "I couldn't sleep," she confessed, her voice soft but weighted with unspoken worries.

In that moment, I felt a surge of vulnerability wash over me, the weight of our shared grief pressing down like a suffocating blanket. "Evelyn, I don't know how to fix this," I admitted, my voice trembling with uncertainty. "Between us, I mean. Can I fix this?"

Tears welled in Evelyn's eyes, her facade of strength crumbling in the face of raw emotion. "Alex, Jacob was the heart of our family," she choked out, her voice thick with sorrow. "Losing him... it's like trying to mend a shattered vase with glue. No matter how hard you try, it'll never be the same."

As the first light of dawn filtered through the window, casting a soft glow over our tear-stained faces, we knew it was time to confront the darkness that threatened to consume us. With heavy hearts and trembling hands, we woke Donovan and Crissy, steeling ourselves for the final showdown with the man who had torn our lives apart.

11 - Sting Operation

As we all gathered for Mayor Caidwall's grand reveal, Donovan was like a maestro conducting an orchestra, getting us all in position for our roles. Crissy, with her trademark wit, couldn't resist making a joke about being the designated distraction. "Why am I always the one who has to be the flashy distraction? Can't I ever be the stealthy spy sneaking in the shadows?"

Donovan laughed, his amusement contagious. "Hey, Crissy, you're the star of the show! Besides, with your flair for the dramatic, who else could pull it off?"

I joined in on the banter, feeling the tension ease a bit. "Yeah, Crissy, you're our secret weapon. Plus, who else could steal the spotlight like you do?"

Crissy rolled her eyes, but there was a playful glint in them. "Alright, alright, I'll take one for the team. But you guys owe me big time for this."

As we continued to prepare, I couldn't help but turn to Donovan with a question that had been on my mind. "Donovan, don't you wanna have a face-to-face with your old man? This is your chance to give him a piece of your mind."

He paused, a thoughtful look crossing his face. "You know, Alex, I've thought about it. But as much as I'd love to give him a piece of my mind, I want him to face the music for what he's done. When the cops haul him away, that's when I'll get my moment. I'll have a few choice words for him then."

His determination was clear, and I couldn't help but admire his resolve. In that moment, I knew we were all in this together, ready to take down the man who had caused us all so much grief.

With each of us playing our part, we were like a well-oiled machine, ready to execute our plan and bring justice to Everhaven. And as we waited for Caidwall's speech to begin, I felt a sense of camaraderie wash over me, knowing that we were all in this fight together.

As for Evelyn, she stood poised at the electronic billboards, ready to unleash the damning evidence of Caidwall's corruption for all to see. Her role was crucial, and I knew she would handle it with the same steely determination that she brought to everything she did.

"Team, Caidwall's here," I called out urgently through the comms, signaling the start of our plan.

Evelyn and Crissy responded in unison, their voices determined. "Copy that, Alex," they replied, ready to execute their respective roles.

As Caidwall stepped onto the stage to deliver his speech, I relayed the information to the team. "Caidwall's up. Let's do this," I said, my voice tinged with nerves.

Crissy wasted no time, launching into her distraction with gusto. "Incoming cavewoman!" she yelled, her voice echoing through the comms as she stormed onto the stage, grabbing a police officer's gun and making a run for it.

Donovan's voice crackled over the comms, his instructions clear. "Alex, get on stage. Evelyn, standby on the billboards."

I hesitated for a moment, my nerves threatening to overwhelm me. "I don't think so, Mayor," I called out, trying to steady my voice as I stepped onto the stage.

Caidwall's eyes locked onto mine, recognition flashing in his gaze. "Not this guy!" he muttered to himself, his expression darkening as he realized the threat I posed.

Despite his orders, the officers were too preoccupied chasing after Crissy to heed his command. The crowd, sensing the tension, began to boo and jeer, urging me to leave the stage.

"Screw it, Evelyn, do it now!" I shouted into the comms, a surge of adrenaline coursing through me as I watched Evelyn flip the switch, illuminating the billboards with evidence of Caidwall's corruption.

As the crowd's laughter turned to murmurs of disbelief, I seized the opportunity to speak out. "Listen to me, people! Caidwall isn't who you think he is. He's killed to get where he is, and he's not above taking down anyone who stands in his way, including Mayor Fairweather."

The crowd then... started laughing? I got confused and thought that the evidence was enough to get Caidwall behind bars. I knew from there that I had a lot of convincing to do. A elderly man yelled out from the crowd, "Mayor Caidwall is going to restore peace to this city!" he yelled out. Another woman chimed in, "Those pictures are clearly made by AI!" she screamed.

Finally, another young guy yelled out, "Mayor Caidwall would never kill anyone!" he said. I looked to Caidwall who had a very big smirk plastered on his face, he thought that my plan was foiled. Everything around me froze, I thought about

Evelyn, Crissy, Jacob, Donovan, Jason, Mom, and what I've learned in the past year.

I then picked up the microphone, and I started speaking, "My name is Alex. Alex Hawthorne, like most of you, I live here in Everhaven. And let's just say, I've learned a lot in the last year. You know, a while ago, someone told me, 'You are not defined by the tragedies of the past, but of trust in the future.'" I said.

"I stand before you today, not as someone who wants to dwell on the wrongdoings of the past, but as someone who believes in the power of peace and unity. This city has been through tough times, and it's natural to carry some scars. But we absolutely cannot let those scars define us."

"I want you all to know that I understand the pain and the struggles we've faced. But I also believe in our collective strength and resilience. Together, we can rise above the darkness and create a future filled with hope, love, and understanding."

"Let's leave behind the divisions and the animosity. Let's build bridges instead of walls. Let's support one another and work towards a community where everyone feels at peace and safe. We have the power to shape our own destiny and create a legacy of peace and harmony. The legacy that Mayor Fairweather wanted so dearly for this city." I said as tears began forming around my eyes.

As I ended my speech, a woman at the front of the crowd began to speak up, "When Fairweather died, crime began to rise. Me and my husband went on a walk and we were mugged. He... He died trying to protect me." she softly said as she began to swell up. I looked to another man, "My son passed away in a gang shootout. He was in a gang; He believed that we needed protection since Fairweather wasn't around anymore. So I beat the man who did it." The man also began crying.

I then looked to the saddest one of all, I looked to a kid at the very front of the crowd. He began to break down, "My- My-My mommy died trying to save me and my little brother from home robbers."

I looked back up to the entire crowd, who were consoling each other, and tears started falling down my eyes. I put the microphone back to my mouth, "I know you all are scared." I said as I looked up to Evelyn on the building above by one of the billboards, tears in her eyes as well, "I'm scared too. However, Mayor Caidwall has been trying to take what makes Everhaven an amazing city away. The peace that Mayor Fairweather's time highlighted in the city, We need to act now. The mayor killed Fairweather, took my family hostage, and killed one of the ones I love. Everhaven's peace isn't achieved by some lousy corrupt mayor, it's achieved by the people. The people are the hearts of this city."

And, with that ended my speech. The crowd started cheering for me, and then out of the blue, Caidwall began to speak up, making the audience quiet down, "Oh, come on! You can't expect me to believe that he's telling the truth! I mean, those pictures are obviously AI!" He exclaimed. However, the crowd didn't let up and started booing him. The police snatched the gun away from Crissy and came on stage to arrest Richard Caidwall. He cursed at the police officers as they put handcuffs on him and took him away. I got down from the stage walking to Donovan who was at the back of the crowd, as I walked, the entire crowd cheered for me louder and louder.

I walked to Donovan who put his hand out for a handshake, "You did it." He said. I slapped his hand away and reached in for a hug and he did too. "*We* did it."

As I reclined from our hug, I saw Crissy running back from the side of the stage, she ran to me and gave me a hug as well. "We did it! We did it!" she exclaimed, reclining from our hug and jumping up and down, I started laughing. Then, I saw Evelyn jogging back from her post with tears in her eyes; she got close to me, to my face, "Evelyn- I-" she interrupted me. She grabbed the back of my head, pulled me in and began kissing me. Shocked and happy, I pulled her in too.

I reclined from the kiss, and peered at Evelyn's eyes, "Does this mean we're good now Barbie?" I said to her, She mildly chuckled, "Don't test your luck, mate." We all then looked to the sight of Caidwall being carried away into the car by the police. Caidwall looked at Donovan and started laughing, "Wow son, I didn't think you had it in you!" He egotistically said, "Guess, I was right about you, you sniveling weak pussy."

"Father, nice to see you again. What did I say last time I saw you? Oh yeah, I'm going to put you behind reinforced metal bars." Donovan said with a smirk on his face. "Bye-bye!" he said. Caidwall growled at him, then he peered at me. He broke off the officer's grip on his wrists and charged at me, sending me into the ground. I held his arms as he tried hitting me. I looked to one of the police officers, "Hey, Officer, will I get arrested if I hit him back?" I said on the ground facing the officer. The officer jokingly looked away, "I ain't see nothing." he said. I looked back at Caidwall, let go of his arms and punched him in the nose. He got up holding his bloody nose, "Shit! My nose!" he yelled. Then, we all took turns delivering a blow. First

I punched him in the stomach, Evelyn slapped him across the face, Donovan socked him in the mouth, and finally, Crissy delivered a blow to the no-no zone. "That's for Jacob." Crissy muttered.

So there I was, basking in the glory of Caidwall being carted off to jail, feeling like a superhero. Then, bam! Phone rings, and it's Ali on the line. "Assalamualaikum, brother Alex, saw your speech," he says all excited. "What'd you think?" I ask. "Alex, I'm proud of you. May Allah bless you on this road that we call life. Ameen," he blesses. "Ameen," I reply, hanging up with a smirk.

I turn to Donovan, still riding the victory high. "City's gonna need a mayor," he declares, eyeing the crowd. After a sec of contemplation, I drop the bomb, "They already have one," I say, giving his shoulder a reassuring squeeze. He gets it, grins, and embraces the responsibility.

Life's nuts, right? From journalist to window-jumping crime fighter – God sure had a funny way of surprising the shit out of me.

Following the events, I took Evelyn and Crissy to my mom's house while Donovan pursued his mayoral aspirations. When Jason stepped out of the house, I parked the car and got out. He immediately charged at me for a hug, and I reciprocated tightly. After introducing him to Evelyn, Jason greeted her with a simple "Hi." Crissy emerged from the car, and Jason exclaimed, "Woah, what's up peanut?" I covered his mouth, reminding him, "Bro, you can't say stuff like that." Removing my hand, Evelyn chuckled, "Like father, like son."

Crissy and Jason exchanged a smile, creating a moment of connection.

12 - Til Death Do Us Part

I woke up to the sweet melody of baby Jacob's morning serenade. Stretching my arms, I casually announced, "Jacob's belting out his greatest hits today." Heading downstairs, there they were – my family. It's been two decades since we toppled Caidwall's corrupt reign.

Mom, may she rest in peace, left us a few years back. I married Evelyn, and Jason tied the knot with Crissy. Their little one, Jacob Jr., was currently orchestrating a symphony of tears.

I plopped down next to Evelyn, who was consoling our little maestro. Crissy was conjuring up some magic in the kitchen. Jason, now a spitting image of me, handed me coffee, joking, "Sorry, Dad, Jacob's got a set of lungs today." As he hugged me, I reassured him, "Don't worry, you were a mini opera singer yourself."

Jason quipped, "Very funny," and darted off to assist Crissy. Suddenly recalling Jason's job in the city council with Mayor Caidwall (the good one, Donovan), I asked, "No work today, son?" He replied, "Nah, Mayor declared a Friday off. Oh, and he says hi to you and Evelyn."

Evelyn, victorious in getting Jacob Jr. to nap, chimed in, "Tell Donovan to drop by sometime." Crissy, calling from the kitchen, needed assistance, and Jason sprinted back, dubbing her "peanut."

Observing the life we built – Jacob Jr. snoozing, Jason on kitchen duty – I marveled, "Where did time fly?" Glancing at Evelyn, I mused, "It feels like just yesterday you aimed a gun at me."

Evelyn chuckled, "And it feels like only yesterday you were yelping like a scaredy-cat." Laughing, I reflected on the twists and turns that brought us here. "Thank you for sticking around – for me, for the family," I expressed, withdrawing my hand from her cheek.

"Till death do us part, right?" she teased. Beaming, I agreed, "Yeah, till death do us part." Then, realizing the day, I added, "It's Friday, isn't it?"

"Oh, right! It's Friday," I exclaimed, a sudden realization hitting me. "I've got to head to the mosque for Friday Prayers." I informed the family, giving Evelyn a quick peck on the cheek. "I'll be back soon."

Setting off on foot, I strolled through the familiar streets. As I walked, I spotted my friend Ali up ahead. "Salaam, Ali! How are you?" I greeted him warmly.

Ali grinned, returning the greeting, "Wa Alaikum Salaam! I'm doing well, Alex. How's the family?" We fell into step together, catching up on the happenings of our lives.

We reminisced about the days gone by, sharing stories and laughter. The mosque loomed ahead as our conversation continued. "It's always good to catch up, Ali. We should do this more often," I suggested.

Ali nodded, "Absolutely, Alex. Maybe we can plan something with the families soon." As we reached the mosque, our paths diverged temporarily. "Give me a minute, let me do Wudhu" Ali said as he entered the washroom inside.

Entering the mosque, I found solace in the familiar rituals of Friday Prayers. The serenity of the place offered a moment of reflection amidst life's bustling pace.

After the prayers, I found a quiet corner for some heartfelt dua, seeking guidance and gratitude. As I was deep in reflection, Ali joined me, taking a seat beside me.

Silently contemplating, I finally asked, "Do you ever wonder if your life has made a difference?" Ali looked at me with understanding eyes, "Alex, every life is significant. We're all valued and loved by God."

His words resonated with me as he continued, "You, my friend, have lived your purpose – exposing corruption, bringing light where there was darkness." I nodded, a mix of emotions flooding in.

"Thank you for being there through all these years," I expressed my gratitude. Ali smiled warmly, "It's been an honor, Alex. But remember, if you want to leave a lasting legacy, spread messages of love and respect. Give what was given to you."

As our conversation wrapped up, Ali stood up, mentioning he had to head home. "See you soon, my friend," he said, leaving me with a renewed sense of purpose and a heart full of gratitude for the meaningful connections in my life.

As I finished my dua, my eyes wandered across the mosque, and there, in a corner, I noticed a little boy curled up, tears streaming down his face as he whispered his own prayers. Moved by empathy, I walked over and gently placed a hand on his shoulder.

"Hey, everything okay, buddy?" I asked, crouching down beside him. The boy looked up, his eyes still wet, and hesitant but shared the worries that burdened his little heart.

The little boy poured out his heart, sharing a weight that seemed far too heavy for his small shoulders. He spoke of his perceived sins, each word laden with guilt. "I've done so many bad things. I don't know how God could ever forgive me," he confessed, his eyes reflecting a deep sense of remorse.

Kneeling beside him, I listened attentively, understanding the weight of his words. I offered a gentle response, "Hey, we all make mistakes, big or small. But you know, God is the most forgiving. He sees the goodness in our hearts and loves us despite our flaws."

The boy looked up, his eyes searching for reassurance. "But what if I keep messing up?" he questioned, his voice tinged with worry. I shared a comforting smile, "We're all a work in progress, kiddo. God's mercy is endless. He understands our struggles and forgives us when we sincerely seek forgiveness."

As the little one continued to pour out his heart, the realization hit me, this boy was me. Me, 20 years ago; the state of emotions I was in and how badly I messed up, "Woah, this is like, a full circle moment." I muttered under my breath.

"What?" The boy said. I fixed myself up, "No, nothing. Look, that guilt you feel when you sin. That's your love for Allah persevering, like I said, Allah knows your struggles, he knows your intentions." I said as I began to remember the talk Ali gave me all those years ago, "Surround yourself with stuff that pleases Allah, so that you may move away from sinning."

I then dropped the exact bombshell that Ali dropped on me 2 decades ago, "Someone once told me that, 'You are not defined by the tragedies of the past; but of trust in the future.' Just because you think you've sinned too much, doesn't mean that Allah doesn't forgive you. He has a future planned for you, one filled with happiness only if you place your trust into him."

The boy's eyes swelled up even more, "Thank you, sir." The boy said as we began to stand up, "Hawthorne, but you can call me Alex. I don't really care for formalities." I stated.

As the boy dashed off, gratitude etched across his face, I couldn't help but wonder once again: had our efforts truly made a difference? The question echoed in my mind as I made my way home, lost in thought.

Reflecting on my journey, I remembered the battles fought, the evil regimes toppled, and the moments of doubt where I thought I'd lost myself forever. But somehow, against all odds, I found my way back to the path of righteousness.

After a brisk walk, I reached home, my mind still grappling with the weight of my ponderings. Through the window, I spotted Crissy, engrossed in her work at the desk. Catching sight of me, she flashed a bright smile and waved eagerly.

"Hey, Dad's back!" she exclaimed, her voice carrying through the house as she bounded from her desk.

And then, in that ordinary moment, something extraordinary happened. It was a simple gesture, but it spoke volumes. It was a reminder that amidst the chaos and uncertainty, there was still love and warmth waiting for me at home. And as Crissy welcomed me with open arms, I couldn't help but feel a surge of gratitude for the family that stood by me through thick and thin.

Then, *it* happened.

I heard the purr of a car engine; I looked behind me and a black jeep pulled along the curb. And a man in a black suit stepped out of a vehicle, he walked towards me and stopped. "Alex Hawthorne?" The man said with a deep and disgruntled voice.

I looked at him in confusion, "Yeah, that's me." I said as I fixed my posture. The man then pulled out a pistol and aimed it at me. I knew exactly why he was here, "Richard Caidwall sends his regards."

He shot me in the heart and drove away. I felt my world collapse around me as I fell to the ground, bleeding out. The whole family heard the gunshot and surrounded me. Crissy, Jason, and Evelyn. They all started crying and screaming, while neighbors watched in shock. "No! God, please no!" Evelyn screamed. I held Evelyn's hands, "It's okay." I said as I looked at my beautiful family. "It's going to be just, okay."

I felt myself slipping from this world, "I love you all." My world went black.

Our lives are like a canvas painted with challenges and victories, the stuff that molds us into who we are. Be it taking on corruption or comforting a weeping child in a mosque, every move, whether grand or tiny, leaves a lasting impression on the masterpiece of our existence.

And hey, no matter what unfolds, just hold onto trust. Trust in the big guy upstairs, trust in your loved ones, and most of all, trust that the future's got something good in store.

Author's Note

One of my absolute favorite movies is *Marvel's X-Men Days Of Future Past*. The movie is centered around how this team of super powered heroes must go back in time to prevent an assassination that dooms the future of these super powered people. One of the main and recurring themes in that movie is the power of redemption. There's a quote from the movie that has become essential to who I am as a person, the quote is,

"Just because someone stumbles, loses their way, it doesn't mean they're lost forever."

This quote is said by Patrick Stewart's character: Charles Xavier. This quote is very important as it shows that people may stumble sometimes. However, it doesn't mean that they are a lost cause, get up, try again, and trust that your situation will become better. I found that me and Alex were alike... not that I snuck into government buildings or took down a corrupt politician. But the fact that, I was lost at one point in my life, I felt like I was a horrible person and that I brung everyone down when I was near them. When my dad passed away, these feelings of self doubt amplified themselves and I just fell into a slumber. I kept feeling sorry for myself. One of my uncles, we'll call him, Uncle Devon. Uncle Devon and his brother, my other uncle; they both showed me the beauty and power of religion, the power of Islam. Suddenly, the hole in my heart, the "broken pieces" started coming together, I felt happier, and more grateful. I felt like I didn't need to pretend to smile around my family and friends.

In this book, we see Alex go on a self-discovery journey as he learns who he is as a person and who he is to the people around him. Alex betrays his friends, and it leads him down a dark path of cutting his son out, and relying on drinking. However, he learns that trusting in the future and God, that it's going to be alright.

And that's what I'm here to tell you, that everything is going to be alright, rely on others, let yourself fall and get picked up by the ones you love.

Another thing I tried to emphasize in this story, is that the messages that we leave in our wake will always remain even if we don't. To have trust in the future, you must also give the future messages and ideas to live by.

If you take anything from my life story, or this book: let it be the fact that whatever tragedy that falls upon you that's too tough or stressful for you, let yourself be vulnerable, let yourself be picked up by the ones you love, and just trust that the future holds something pure for you because,

"You are not defined by the tragedies of the past; but of trust in the future."

Yours Sincerely,
Zayn Jamshaid

About the Author

Zayn Jamshaid, a 16-year-old aspiring writer, faces numerous challenges as he strives for success. Zayn went through numerous challenges when he was young, which had an impact on his life, but he didn't allow that stop him from enjoying writing, spending time with family, reading comic books, playing video games, and practicing his spirituality.

Milton Keynes UK
Ingram Content Group UK Ltd.
UKHW020732010424
440421UK00014B/764

9 798224 117505